AF489655

AFTER

COMMENCEMENT

A Debut Novel

by

Michael J. Consolmagno Jr.

AFTER
COMMENCEMENT

A Novel

MICHAEL J. CONSOLMAGNO JR.

ISBN: 979-8-9956898-0-5 (Paperback) / ISBN: 979-8-9956898-1-2 (Hardcover) / ISBN: 979-8-9956898-2-9 (E-Book)

Library of Congress Control Number: 2026909654

The story, all names, characters, and incidents portrayed in this production are fictitious. No identification with actual persons (living or deceased), places, buildings, and products is intended or should be inferred.

Front Cover Design by April Consolmagno

1st edition 2026

Published by Great Counsel Entertainment

Staten IsIsland, NY

For my sister,

Tara

Without whom this story couldn't be told

CONTENTS

ONE

SPRING COMMENCEMENT

The shoes are a size ten. Joseph, who's worn a size ten since he turned eighteen, feels them pinch his feet as he perches above his graduating class.

In his dorm room earlier, they seemed fine. Now, they're tight. These particular shoes, despite being the same fit as numerous other options, are his chosen pair for the day.

They weren't picked to match the bright green gown or smartly complement the tan khakis underneath. On the contrary, they're excessively flashy, gaudy relics at least a decade out of style. Still, he swore to wear them, and tight or not, they remain fastened to his feet.

He obsesses and spins his ill-fitting gold college ring around his finger, letting his focus drift from the moment.

Michigan State University's Breslin Center, a 15,000-seat arena nestled south of the Red Cedar River, buzzes with the eager murmur of spring graduates and their families. The Spartans, who clinched a spot in the NCAA Final Four six weeks back in March, call this court home. Today, it's trading basketball games for caps and gowns. Sunlight streams through high windows, glinting off green-and-white banners that sway gently in the air-conditioned breeze. The polished hardwood, usually alive with the squeak of sneakers, lies hidden beneath a temporary stage, while the crowd's whispers mingle with the rustle of programs and distant cheers.

Steps from the university president and tenured bigwigs, Joseph sits among the honorees for the May 1999 Grand Convocation. The podium looms before him, the microphone gleaming under the arena's lights, his stomach knotting as the distance seems to stretch with each passing second.

It feels unreal, an impossible dream with only the tightness of his shoes keeping him grounded.

Elie Wiesel, renowned author and Holocaust survivor, warns the young men and women in attendance about the perils of indifference toward global events. His tone is unwavering but polite and commanding. Close by, Joseph strains to catch it, but a mounting panic drowns the words as fast as they slip from Mr. Wiesel's mouth.

He's next. Following a Nobel Prize laureate, using the same microphone that carried a voice unbroken by humanity's darkest moments. Joseph's fingers tremble as he grips the paper, his speech feeling flimsy now.

Backstage, he shook the gentleman's hand, introduced himself, and mentioned how his grandfather fought in World War II. A quick greeting that felt important at the time, blank now as Mr. Wiesel wraps up.

Joseph clutches his pages tighter, the lines he made sure to memorize darkening. His vision blurs, his thoughts turn muddy, and his feet won't stop throbbing.

Was that my name? He jerks up, an outstretched hand beckoning him to the podium. Smiles gleam, and polite claps echo from the attendees. Joseph realizes it's meant for him. No more stalling; his moment's here, and everything is about to commence.

Joseph stands, nerves jarring him forward. Each step drags, then lightens as the mic nears. He recalls this feeling well. A rush of adrenaline mixed with a gut twist. It's the old high school track meet anxiety. Mr. Wiesel places his hand gently on his shoulder.

"Good luck, son. They're all yours," his firm smile leading the young graduate toward the spotlight. Joseph nods, hoping his face mirrors the sentiment, but he's half here. Recognizing the words and witnessing the gentleman's smile but remaining adrift in the shadows of the stage lights. Joseph musters up a thank you, unsure of how it lands.

At the podium, he slips off his loose ring, *can't risk it fumbling free,* and carefully sets it by his speech. He nudges the microphone up to a comfortable height, his eyes hitting the crowd.

The weight of the commencement honor rocks him; a sea of patient eyes, fellow graduates spreading out, sparks a jolt inside. He hunts for his loved ones among the green glare of bodies, but nothing sticks out. Still, he can feel them out there, the ones this day is really for, the ones he wants to make proud: his family.

Knowing they're watching cuts through the fog. His head clears, his sight snaps sharp, and the aching in his feet decides to quit. The gun's about to be fired, and he's crouched on the starting blocks. He has to be.

"Thank you, Mr. Wiesel," Joseph starts, his voice a touch thicker than he intends.

"Wow, okay, just give me a moment," he stalls, allowing himself time to rub at his throat.

Grabbing the loose paper containing his address from the podium, Joseph turns it over. The words ripen, vivid as the day he'd scratched them down.

He never truly believed he'd be the one to stand here, to receive this duty. It seemed like a long shot, a speech dedicated to his family, delivered to a graduating class of one of the world's largest institutions. Surely it was too raw, too intimate; he was positive they'd toss it. Yet it clicked. Somehow, it was found worthy, and he got the nod. Now, the time to share his heart embedded in the ink arrives.

"Hello! First off, let me say congratulations once again. Instead of having you sit there, wondering who this guy is, let me introduce myself. My name is Joseph Vitagliano, and I'm one of you, a graduate. That's for the people who the cap and gown didn't give it away."

Soft laughter ripples through the audience, easing Joseph's jitters. He continues, his tone warm and conversational, engaging the crowd.

"Now that we've gotten the pleasantries out of the way, let me begin. I could stand up here all day and give you words of advice and points of wisdom, talk about what you should do with your lives, and set goals for the future. However, I won't, because mainly that wouldn't be fair to you or me. And, well, they'll cut the microphone off in five minutes."

Chuckles grow, spreading out like a wave. Joseph pauses, nerves loosening, allowing the laughter to subside.

"Instead, I'd like to tell you a little bit about myself and what graduating from Michigan State University means to me. I hope my words are at the very least something you can empathize with, if not relate to," he scans his classmates, connecting eye to eye with each passing glance.

In late August of 1994, he hit the campus cocky, prepared to own it. He'd been determined to make the best of his college experience. But little did he know his decision to attend MSU would create a divide in his life, one part here and the other 700 miles away in Staten Island, New York, his home.

At the mention of New York, Joseph hears a spattering of applause, veering him off-script. "Oh, good, we can clap for New York," he quips, grins breaking out. "So, while I was here making new friends, stressing over grades, and falling in love with my beautiful girlfriend, Bella..."

An "aww" rises from the audience, and Joseph's cheeks flare red. The acknowledgment of Bella pulls him back to their first meeting, a memory as vivid as the glowing lights. Joseph was supposed to have his own room for the first time ever. He became an RA, drawn primarily by the free room and board, and was excited to settle into having no more roommates for the remainder of his time at school. Things were going great for about a day until the freshmen started moving into the dorms. The boys on floor 3, being the wholesome, welcoming souls they were, traveled to the all-girls section above to greet the new arrivals and welcome them. Each door adorned with name tags, two per room: Jennie and Nicole, Sarah and Jamie, Saffron and Michele, and, at room 405, Bella and Deena. Joseph knocked on the door to the last thing he expected, a sight of home. Her familiar Mediterranean features, paler than those back east, struck a comfortable chord in his heart. Bella laughed at his accent, and he knew he was done for. By a month into the fall semester, they unofficially shared his quarters, sleeping soundly together on his Spider-Man bedsheets, watched over by his Spawn poster. Joseph found himself once again without a room of his own, but for the first time, he didn't mind it.

Joseph shakes off the recollection, his smile lingering as he faces the crowd. He's loose now, the audience is in his hands, and he knows it.

"...my family and all those who helped me get here started changing and growing without me. I mean, who do they think they are?" he cracks, letting his East Coast accent shine through. "But still, I decided to stay and finish what I started because being a graduate of Michigan State is worth it to me."

He recalls his initial moments on campus, the vast and striking differences that greeted him. Years blur together, but certain details crystallize: a particular tree swaying on a sunny day, ducks dawdling along the Red Cedar. It was impossible not to fall in love with the intangible aura of the school, a feeling he was sure would remain with him always.

"However, today means more than the time I spent here or the tuition costs that I've paid; well, *they're* not completely paid yet," Joseph quips, glancing back at the university president. A knowing raise of the eyebrows sparks guffaws from the crowd.

"Its value instead lies in what I've sacrificed and what I missed by being here. I come from a moderately large family that doesn't just include my parents and my siblings, but also my aunts, uncles, cousins, and grandparents," he states, eyes roving, hopeful.

"I grew up with them always around, always offering their support. And before I came to MSU, not a day would go by where I didn't interact with them. So, what I'm trying to tell you is that we're a family in the truest sense of the word," he adds, full-voiced, proud.

He hunts again for his loved ones in the green expanse in front of him. Unable to locate them, he glances toward the sky, then back to the bustling arena.

"So, I was the first to go away to college, and it was tough for me," he confesses, strain creeping in. "When I left, my older cousins weren't married, never mind my best friend, Ezra. My brothers weren't even shaving. Simply put, there were just too many little things in their everyday lives that I wasn't a part of, and I wasn't there for them if they needed me for anything."

He stops, catching nods from faces that seemingly share this bittersweet heartache.

"I could call them, and I often did, but every time I got off the phone, I would feel that much further away and that much more alone," he admits, his voice fading into his past.

"So, every winter break and every summer, my flight home left two hours after my last final, and my flight back here landed two hours before my first class," Joseph recounts, steeling his resolve for the touchy bit ahead. "Except for one time, last summer when I decided to take summer classes," his voice cracks, startling him, and he hurriedly collects himself.

"On that summer night, around 12:15 AM on June 3rd, I was awoken..." Wetness glints in his eyes. "I was awoken by a phone call, telling me to come home, that my grandfather had died," throat parched, he pauses. The room hushes, the air static and still.

Joseph nods at the quiet, forcing a swallow and an exhale. He locks in his resolve and continues, "I came home from the funeral, and my mother told me the stories of what happened. I sat there with my sister, who was also away at a university at that time, sharing the pain and the guilt that I know we both felt from not being there."

Aware that his family was out among the crowd but resolutely believing in the importance of conveying his experience, he weighs their take on spilling this fresh hurt with strangers.

"But still, I stand here before you, wearing my grandfather's shoes, to tell you that it was worth it," he says, taking in the leather at his feet, digging more into his mind than his body.

Applause swells, a recognition of the small sacrifices each may have made to receive their degrees.

"It's up to me, and me alone, to make my degree worth so much more," Joseph pushes, determined to finish strong.

"And as I stand here before you, I remember certain things that were said to me before I got here. In particular, my godfather, my Uncle Luke, came to me and said, *This is what your grandfather wanted when he came to America. You are a fulfillment of his dreams.*"

Joseph rests, letting the occasion sink in. Narrowing his focus, he asserts with a voice that bellows from the speakers, "But more than what he said, *this* is a fulfillment of my dreams as well."

"So, let me end on this last thought," Joseph's voice climbs. "I hope you all realize the worth of this moment and the privilege that we all now share. And please, if you do nothing else, make it mean that much more every day of your lives."

Applause fills the Breslin Center, a resounding affirmation of his words.

As it subsides, Joseph stands tall, his heart full of gratefulness. He slides his ring back on, its heft a reminder of the prior five years, and yet, despite the win, the old track meet butterflies reappear. The ring begins to slip, so he closes his fist, gripping it tight, preventing it from dropping to the ground. He knows this milestone is only the beginning, but a worry darkens it: thoughts about what fresh sacrifices he was going to make and what he was now forsaking to return home.

Brooklyn was the old country. It seemed like every-one from Staten Island originally came from its streets. Joseph was born in an area called Gravesend, but he wasn't really raised there. Still, as an Italian kid from New York, his Brooklyn roots remained. Throughout his years in Michigan, his friends, oblivious to the five-borough hierarchy of New York City, nicknamed him Brooklyn. Some never even knew his real name was Joseph, a fact that amused his father, Joseph Sr., himself a proud son of Gravesend.

Upon Joseph Sr.'s arrival at the dorm, his son's college buddies freeze. Most of their experience with Americans of Italian descent limited to pop-culture caricatures. Their Midwestern minds struggle to reconcile him with the mafioso stereotypes they've seen on screen. At five-five with a barrel chest and piercing blue eyes, Joseph Sr. owns the room, capturing the Spartans' attention as they bid their farewells. Packing up like a pro, his father crams Joseph's entire collegiate life into the family van.

Joseph stands in his dorm room for the final time, the best part of the last five years wraps her arms around him. Ever so softly, he brushes the hair from her face, tucking it behind her ear. Surprised by the tear he finds on her cheek, he kisses it gently away, then kisses her deeply.

"I love you." A whisper, small and profound in the quiet of the empty room. The last one to be shared in their space, belonging now among the ghosts of past utterances. They hold hands and say no more as they make their way to the exit.

As he drives off, Joseph's view of the dorm smudges. His gaze fixes on Bella, his girl, standing motionless, waiting to see if the car will turn around. *It never does. It never even slows.* Joseph's chest tightens as the packed van continues to roll on its journey toward the Atlantic and away from her.

"There's a stranger in my house
It took a while to figure out
There's no way you could be
Who you say you are,
you gotta be someone else"
-Tamia

Two

STRANGER IN MY HOUSE

A week gone by, and the goodbyes keep replaying in Joseph's mind. Living in Staten Island still means keeping one foot in the old country. The sunlight reflects off the Verrazano-Narrows Bridge connecting the two. Over the hundreds of crossings in his lifetime, he would crane his neck, watching its archways fly overhead. But today, in the backseat of a tan 1995 Nissan Altima, he isn't looking to the heavens. Instead, he peers out the side window, catching a glimpse of Lady Liberty standing stiff in her harbor, perpetually waiting.

The van's engine trouble puzzles him; he isn't sure what happened, but as the person operating it when the yellow warning light came on, he wants to help bring it in for an inspection. His uncle lives on the island, but his auto body shop is where else? Brooklyn. Driving solo, the ride in was quiet, and now, even with his parents in the front, the trip back passes in a similar silence.

Before setting out, Joseph Sr. called an old jeweler he knew from the neighborhood. After the van's drop-off at his uncle's, they detoured down a familiar avenue; memories like grease-smeared glass flickered in Joseph's mind. The jeweler, a friendly Jewish man with long, curled sideburns and a black yarmulke, gave his father a firm handshake, his eyes crinkling with a smile. He slipped Joseph's finger into a sizer, and Joseph removed his college ring from a pocket and placed it into the stranger's hand. As it was carried to the back, Joseph's gut twisted at abandoning it. The jeweler promised Joseph Sr. updates and even offered to mail it back.

Brooklyn was his father's home, where he knew the faces, the grind, and the unwritten rules. The street's secrets, only true locals understood, burned into him.

Now stalling in traffic, waiting to pay the toll, Joseph spots dents in his dad's armor, nothing jarring, just tiny glimpses of the man underneath his brick wall of paternity. Someone tested, shaped by choices and compromises, the small, uncomfortable decisions chasing a better tomorrow for those he loves. His escape from the old country to the new.

The Altima decelerates, Joseph Sr. tosses the exact change into the basket, and rolls past the "Welcome to Staten Island" sign. He accelerates onto the Richmond Parkway, veers right to the exit ramp, and stops briefly at Fine Fare.

Joseph trails his mother through the labyrinth of grocery aisles, helping her toss what feels like the entire store into their shopping cart. Angie moves with the precision of a seasoned navigator, her pace quick and purposeful, as if the layout of Fine Fare is etched into her DNA. Joseph shadows her, pushing the cart beneath the steady hum of the fluorescent lights overhead. He's never seen his mom with his Game Boy; Tetris wasn't her thing, but watching her fit each item into the overflowing cart with impossible efficiency, he's convinced she'd be a natural. By the time they reach the produce section, the cart brims with a mountain of groceries. Joseph marvels at how she keeps it all in order, a habit she's had since she was a kid.

Angie, too, was a child of Brooklyn, running the apartment in her family's cramped walk-up while her parents worked and her older sister dodged chores. It's a rhythm she's never shaken, one that drew her at twelve to her future husband's broad shoulders, handsome grin, and guitar strums. Watching him play the day away, his voice smoother than those on the radio, she was convinced he'd become famous. His sprawling family's acceptance of her, with grandparents who tended gardens and a mother and father whose love infused the air like Sunday supper, offered everything her own life had lacked. She dreamed it would be her fairy-tale escape, a break from the burdens thrust upon her, but history, as it often does, found a way to repeat itself.

The Nissan pulls into the arms of Sinclair Avenue. Filled with semi-connected houses and familiar curbs, it draws a smile potent enough to knock the worry from Joseph's mind.

On his seventh birthday, the Vitaglianos closed on their new house. Nestled at the end of a tidy row of townhouses, it stood quietly distinct in the middle of the block. The house boasted a slightly larger front yard than its neighboring homes, not as expansive as the detached ones nearby, but just enough to lend it a subtle distinction in the tight-knit sprawl.

The house spanned three floors: the upstairs held three bedrooms, the ground floor featured the living areas and kitchen, and the basement served as a space for the boys and casual hangouts. Perched on a gentle slope, the home welcomed visitors through an entrance that opened into the living/dining room. Just past it sat the kitchen, and through the sliding glass doors at the rear was a balcony overlooking the fenced-in backyard below. Beneath it, with its own pair of sliding doors, was the finished basement, offering seamless access to the backyard and blending indoor comfort with easy passage to the pool, which was framed by a wooden deck and a concrete patio.

Even after they moved in during Joseph's third-grade year, the family continued their daily odyssey back to Gravesend for school before accepting his Staten Island baptism the following September.

The Altima's trunk creaks open. Angie heads to the front door with the first grocery bag, while Joseph and his father engage in a silent duel, testing the limit of how many plastic handles they can carry on one wrist.

Angie enters the cramped surroundings of her once-pristine parlor. Her deep brown eyes, shared by her two older boys, take in a sight she'd rather forget. In lieu of the organized lower middle-class home she painstakingly maintains, she meets a clutter of milk crates and lock chests. Five years of her son's college career; posters, tchotchkes, and mementos; occupy her sanctuary. The pile blocks her lacquered black china cabinet, zebra-striped loveseat, and matching couch, gnawing at her space and her patience. In the span of seven days, her irritation has morphed from minor annoyance into migraine-inducing *agita.*

Adjacent to her living room, distinguished only by a subtle shift in ambiance, is her dining room. The absence of walls allows the spaces to bleed into each other. It's here, at her cream-colored dining room table with matching chairs, that she finds her sons, Lucas and Anthony. They have a portable radio blaring out a bootlegged Jonathan Peters CD and are dealing a game of poker to Lucas's friends, Jared and Frisco.

"Your Sister's Ass!" Frisco exclaims, slamming his cards down. The sleeves of his NY Rangers jersey tremble, and he shifts the toothpick in his mouth from right to left, his dark hair gleaming with gel under the overhanging light.

Lucas leans forward, eyes on Frisco's hand. "What? What! Why? What did you have?" Lucas asks, his voice spiking.

Frisco, his brown eyes sparkling with mischief, smiles. "Forget it," he says, turning his head. "I don't even want to show."

The boys groan, flinging their hands in the air.

Angie grins, soaking in the atmosphere. She relishes making her home welcoming, getting to know her children's friends, and using it to gauge their trustworthiness. Over the last few years, these young men have eaten at her table and joined her on car rides back and forth from games, their chatter and laughter spilling through open windows. She's dropped them off for parties and dates, watching them grow until they earned licenses of their own. She's met their families, shared in memories, and even navigated their occasional *doot-da-doo* moments. They were good boys, and she's proud knowing her children chose their company wisely. *Proof she's nailing it.*

After high school, Lucas left his Stony Brook scholarship behind to remain local at the College of Staten Island. So many of Lucas's fellow graduates from Tottenville High attend the college that they've taken to calling it Tottenville Number 2. The proximity allows the crew to stay tight, and due to their constant presence in her home, Angie feels like she's gained permanent residents.

But scanning Joseph's mess in her home, her mood sours. Her eldest son appears to have hit a snag in reconnecting with old friends. She reminds herself it's not her business; he'll figure it out. *He made solid choices, too, once.*

"Lucas, Tony, come help your father with the bags," Angie calls, cutting their game short.

Lucas, his ribbed white guinea tee taut across his torso, crosses his well-muscled arms and stays put.

"Where the hell have you been?" he exclaims, throwing his hands up. "I had to go to soccer practice earlier, but there was no car around. I missed it."

She blanks. Juggling the household is harder now. When Joseph was away, routines were simpler, balanced. She'd even lost a few pounds. Now things were different. The daily task of discerning which son needs what thing requires recalibration. It was much easier when they were young, but they were no longer so small.

Anthony, her baby, is already 15. Her last bundle of joy, hideous on arrival, but now handsome enough to turn heads. At his birth, she was so aghast at his appearance she wasn't sure she was handed the right child, her sister-in-law leaning in, "Don't worry, he'll change," and thank the Lord he did. Square jaw, raven hair, and her husband's crystal blue eyes. He is her angel. Angie's wrangling men now, not boys.

Anthony, the peacemaker, slips out to assist with the bags, avoiding the brewing clash.

Angie knows she forgot her promise but skips excuses; there's no point, it's too late to make a difference anyway. She hammers in on the help she needs now.

"Don't yell at me! Take the bus. We needed the car."

Lucas, frustrated, spits, "Don't be a wiseass. If I had my own car, we wouldn't have to go through this." His words bite. Her little boy, who once entertained her with puppet shows, now hurls insults.

No matter; Angie won't crack. Throughout her life, she's choked down worse disrespect to keep her family strong, whether from her upbringing and the demands of her parents or the growing disillusionment of her son.

"Shut up and go help with the bags," she commands. Sensing her fuse shortening, Frisco intervenes.

"I'll help, Angie," he rises from his seat and hurries outside. Lucas sulks into the kitchen, seeking calm in a glass of iced tea.

Joseph crosses the doorway with a full load of groceries and goes straight to the kitchen. He places them on the glass table before heading back out.

Joseph Sr. meets him, his gaze falling on the card game. Lucas emerges, grimacing at his father's widening eyes.

"You're playing cards in my house," Joseph Sr. barks. "What did I tell you? I don't want gambling in my house."

The Vitaglianos were no wise guys, but with a Teamster father and performing music in Brooklyn since the '60s, Joseph Sr., of course, knew them. They paid well, and he sometimes enjoyed their company, but he never considered any of them friends.

Drug use, loan sharking, and shakedowns. He'd witnessed all types fall into the traps of bad choices, each one starting small, and he adheres to a strict moral code, refusing to watch his sons go down the same path.

"Did you go to soccer practice?"

"How could I?" Lucas snaps. "There was no car."

"You could have taken the bus, Lucas," Joseph Sr. replies, eyes narrowing into hard slits.

Lucas mutters "wiseass" under his breath.

Anger flares in Joseph Sr., old muscles tightening, street-fight instincts flashing. *"What?* Who do you think you are, talking to me that way?"

Frisco and Anthony enter, arms full of bags. Anthony heads straight to the kitchen; Frisco, sensing the tension, creeps in.

Playing dumb, he asks, "Where should I put these?"

Joseph Sr. shoos Frisco toward the kitchen with a wave. "Put them on the counter in there."

Angie brushes through, hurrying past her husband. If she notices the charged air in the room, she keeps a lid on it. Groceries aren't going to put themselves away, another thankless task to hold her house together. Frisco drops the bags down and quickly goes back for more.

Joseph pauses him at the doorway. "This is the last of them," he announces, thrusting the final grocery bag into Frisco's hands. Frisco nods and carries it toward the kitchen. As he scurries by Jared, he casts a fleeting glance his way. Jared catches the hint and springs into action. His hazel eyes dart around the table, and he scoops up the red plastic tokens and playing cards scattered across it, tucking them back into their battered shoebox, each piece finding its proper position.

Lucas's ears burn crimson in his older brother's presence. For the past five years, since he turned fourteen to now, he's enjoyed having the house to himself. Sure, Anthony was around, but he was simply the baby, easily dismissed.

This space, this house, is Lucas's. His older siblings returned for Christmas and the summer, but those were brief pop-ins, a quick you see them, quick you don't type of deal. Now, here's Joseph, his garbage filling up his living room, intruding on his house, sleeping in his bedroom, encroaching on his comfort, and disrupting his life.

Lucas vents at his father. "The best part is, I go to grab my soccer bag this morning, and there are all toys in it! I couldn't find my cleats..."

"They're probably in the cleat bag," Joseph adds.

Lucas's eyebrows shoot up, and he turns to his brother. *He didn't just hear what he thought he did, did he?* The words bounce in his skull, and he can't help but repeat them, "Cleat bag?"

Even as they're said aloud, they still make no sense to him. *What the fuck is a cleat bag?*

"Yeah, the closet was a mess, so I cleaned and organized it," Joseph explains.

The solution to what's happened to his sporting equipment doesn't cool Lucas off.

"Don't touch my stuff! Now I don't know where... God!" Lucas balls his fist and then splays his fingers open, his arms shake, and his face twists in disgust. "First, I miss practice because I don't have a car..."

Joseph intended to help. The basement closet lacked any logical sorting; it was a shit show. Duffel bags filled to bursting with an assortment of random junk. An amalgamation of old toys, mismatched sports gear, boxes of photos, books, and records haphazardly stacked on top of each other.

Two afternoons ago, Joseph was alone watching television when a stray thought struck him. Perhaps there's a better way to store and organize items than randomly tossing them around. In the space of a few hours, he'd completely rearranged the closet—mission accomplished. The hardest part was finding where to start, and since he already had access to multiple duffel bags, why not use them to put like things with like things?

"I see your friends are here. Why didn't you call them for a ride or take the bus?" Joseph suggests. He sets down the last of the groceries and returns to the living room.

"Don't be a wiseass," Lucas retorts. "And where's the bus? In the bus bag?"

"That's a classic line right there, *bus bag,*" Frisco snorts.

Joseph's irritation spikes at Frisco's laughter. *Who the hell is he to sit at their table, acting like he belongs?*

"You've only been home a week, and already my life is hell," Lucas exclaims. "Instead of touching the closet, why don't you get your stuff out of the living room?"

Joseph can't swallow his brother's ingratitude. Lucas may be a gifted athlete, but when it comes to helping out around the house, he's equally talented at avoiding it.

"Hey, Lou, if you took better care of your things, maybe you'd be able to find them."

Lucas rolls his eyes. Who is Joseph to act superior? He has a system. Chaotic? Yes, but effective. The left grey cleat is strategically hidden under the maroon duffle bag, next to the blue cleats that are a size too small. And the right grey cleat? Well, it's always nearby, waiting to be uncovered with a bit of careful rummaging. Of course, he had to make sure not to mistake them for the old grey sneakers he leaves in there for emergencies. It's Joseph who needs help, not him.

"And if you took your head out of your ass, maybe you'd be able to see," Lucas fires back.

Heat swells in the room. Jared, sensing the vibe shift, kills the radio in the middle of a song.

"Enough!" Joseph Sr. plants himself between the two boys. He understands the dynamics at play and feels for his sons as they navigate the new setup. It's going to take time, but he's sure in his heart it will all work out. However, not this minute, and not anytime soon.

"He's right. You're old enough to take care of your own things, Lucas," he affirms, silencing his son and giving Joseph the pass.

Frisco jumps in, sliding next to Joseph, voice perked. "When's El coming in?"

Joseph finds the question odd. His sister is finishing at Ohio State, taking her last summer session before graduating in August.

He wonders if Frisco's interest in his family is too much. He likes Frisco, thinks he's funny at times, but why is he so attached? After all, Frisco has a younger sibling of his own.

"How's your brother doing?" Joseph questions back. "He's around Anthony's age, right? I've noticed you're here quite often, but you never bring him around."

"Oh, he's not the hang-out type, you know, chubby bastard," Frisco chuckles. "So when is she getting here?"

Joseph sees no harm in answering, although Frisco's delusional if he thinks he has any shot with his sister. Besides, Stella's already with a tall, blonde, blue-eyed guy from Ohio. About as far from the typical Staten Island *cugine* as you can get.

"She'll be here at the end of the summer."

Frisco shakes his head. "Not your sister, your girlfriend?"

The mention of his girlfriend sobers Joseph's foul mood. Since coming home, he's ached for her. And albeit the longing remains, glancing thoughts of her bring a smile.

"Oh, I don't know. We haven't finalized any arrangements yet," he says, a hint of uncertainty creeping in.

Jared, relieved by the calmer tone, joins in. "So, where does your girlfriend live?"

"Michigan."

Jared glances at the green and white memorabilia behind Joseph. "Ah, duh. Long-distance relationship, huh? That's gotta be tough. Good luck with that," he smirks.

Joseph gets the doubt, but his optimism persists. How could it not, with the advancements of technology bridging the gap? Amazingly, a few short months is all that's left of the last year of the millennium. Times are changing rapidly, and while flying cars might not be in every driveway, there are significant improvements to bank on. Beepers, no longer exclusive to businessmen and drug dealers, have become a means of connection for everyone. A 911 code could signal urgency, and a quick 143 sends feelings of love. People are communicating in a way only the 21st century can bring, and with the invention of e-mail, waiting for a letter by post is becoming a thing of the past. Plus, the trusty telephone isn't going anywhere, and now there's one in almost every room of the house. The future holds promise, and Joseph's determined to use its advances to shorten the distance.

"We'll make it work," he assures Jared. No uncertainty this time.

"Get this," Frisco interjects, emphasizing each syllable. "His girlfriend's name is Bella Vitaglio."

Jared shrugs. "Yeah, so?"

"Sister Stella Vitagliano, girlfriend Bella Vitaglio." Frisco slows, highlighting the absurdity, presenting it with his arms like offering a gift. "Vitagliano, Vitaglio, heh."

Jared lets it sink in. "Sounds like a law firm."

"Leave it to the Jew to bring lawyers into it; I'm surprised you didn't say accountants," Frisco quips.

"Nobody with those names is going to be trusted with money unless they're laundering it," Jared snorts.

Joseph's cheeks flush pink. "Yeah, it was weird at first. Every time I saw her name, I couldn't help but think of my sister. I tried to come up with nicknames or pet names to make it less weird." He pauses. "I figured it out, quick."

The crew laughs, sharing an *I bet you did* look.

He did find something cute to call her. She's his Silly-Bear, but that's a private thing, meant only for them. This time last year, they rented an apartment together a block off campus, marking the first summer either had spent away from home. The place was a dingy one-bedroom with faulty plumbing, featuring a small couch squeezed next to an even smaller round table in the sitting area and a kitchenette with scarcely enough counter space for a dish towel. They propped a fan in the window to fend off the heat and shared meals of cucumber sandwiches and take-out. In their closet-sized bedchamber, a mattress on the floor swapped Spider-Man sheets for sensible navy cotton, while Klimt's *The Kiss* replaced Todd McFarlane's *Spawn* as the poster above their makeshift headboard. Like kids playing grown-up, they turned their shack into a castle, and by nightfall, sitting arm in arm on the couch, they built a home.

With a lingering smile, Joseph adds, "You know, I dated all these Midwest girls, and it was alright, but go figure, I ended up finding the only other Italian out there."

Anthony smacks his forehead and furrows his brow. There's something he needs to tell his brother. What was it? He searches his thoughts, and suddenly it clicks.

"Oh, Bella called earlier," he blurts out.

A phone call! Great. Joseph's heart jumps at the news. "When did she call?"

"Yesterday."

I mean, it's only a phone call, no sweat, Anthony thinks. After all, he and his girlfriend, Jackie, talk on the phone all the time, and he never remembers anything they say to each other.

"Yesterday!?" Joseph's eyes dart from the phone to his brother.

Why didn't he say so? Doesn't he have a girlfriend, too? He should know this is important.

"What did she say? Did she leave a message?"

Anthony, unfazed, checks the fridge. "I don't know. Something about moving into a new apartment tomorrow." Unsatisfied, he closes the door empty-handed. "She expects you to call."

The news of Bella's upcoming move adds another layer of complication to their long-distance struggle. He can't shake the image of her watching him drive away, and now, missing her call feels like abandoning her again.

"Tomorrow, meaning today, or tomorrow as in the present tomorrow, meaning today's tomorrow?"

Anthony's mouth drops open, his head tilting to one side. "Huh? I don't know what she meant; she said tomorrow. I left her new number in the kitchen on a napkin," he points to the counter, his mind already moving on to thoughts of hanging out with Jackie.

Joseph's anxiety eases now that there's hope. If he has the number, it's one less obstacle in the way. Refreshed with purpose, he leaps to the pile of papers. *The napkin is going to be here.*

With the matter settled, Anthony's focus shifts to girlfriend time. "Lucas, can you take me to Jackie's?"

Angie skillfully stacks the final can of corn atop another in the under-cabinet. A small surge of pride washes over her as she finishes, and Joseph, noticing, waves a piece of paper at her.

"Mom, have you seen a napkin with a number on it?" His words snap out at her.

A pang of disappointment pricks her. Joseph isn't here to help; he just needs something. His abrupt question about a worthless napkin ticks her off.

"I didn't *touch* anything!" Angie snaps, her jaw tightening.

"I didn't say anything about that. Did you see a napkin with a number on it?" Joseph softens his voice as he clocks her frustration.

Angie knows her boys. She's understood them since she first cradled them in her arms. There's a time for strength and a time for softness.

"There were a bunch of papers here earlier," she says, pointing to an empty spot on the counter. "I think they might be in the garbage."

The endless clutter of socks, keys, and abandoned projects from her men wears her down. The maelstrom of activity would overtake the house; luckily, she regularly picks up after them. She eyes the shoes scattered by the door and the dishes piling in the sink, tasks seemingly beyond their capabilities to manage. She realizes this napkin, mistaken for yet another dirty one, might be in the trash. Garbage day isn't until tomorrow, so there's hope it's still there, nestled among the remnants of old dinners, filthy with stains from sauce and coffee grounds.

Joseph furrows his brow, his right hand rubbing away at his temple as if to forestall a headache. He starts toward the overstuffed receptacle, contemplating his next move.

Lucas chafes at once again playing chauffeur to his younger brother in the Nissan. He knows helping out is the deal he struck to keep using the car, so here he is, pulling out of the driveway with him yet again.

It's a consistent theme now, his parents asking him to shuttle Anthony here and there. And now that Anthony has a girlfriend; *as if he even knew what to do with one;* the demands feel even more taxing. Jackie's a nice enough girl, Lucas thinks, albeit a little too obsessed with his brother. Still, he can't resist calling her *Jack-Ass* instead of *Jackie*, an immature nickname that never fails to bring a smile to his face and a frown to Tony's.

Frisco and Jared make a U-turn and pull up beside him. Frisco leans out of the driver's side window. "Lou, have you shown Joe the Shelley Tape?"

A muscle jumps in Lucas's cheek; unable to figure out why Frisco is dragging Joseph into their business. Joseph doesn't know a damn thing about Lucas's life, anything about his friends, or who Shelley even is, and Lucas is perfectly fine with keeping it that way.

"No, he doesn't even know her."

Frisco nods, a mischievous grin spreading. "That's N. G. on the tape. I'll have to show him later."

Frisco's car pulls away. Jared, seated in the passenger seat, turns toward him, shoulders dropping. "Angie? Who's Angie? Mrs. V?"

Frisco chuckles. "Not Angie, N! G!"

Jared tilts his head back. "Oh."

With the tape fresh in his mind, Frisco pokes Jared. "You saw the tape, right?"

Jared's nostrils flare, his mouth agape. "Yeah, I saw it."

Frisco taps the steering wheel, a gutsy cackle kicking up his throat. "Keeeeeee. Come on, I don't care; it's funny."

Jared's scowl deepens, his disgust growing. There's history between Jared and Shelley, and Frisco knows it. Still, Frisco can't help himself; he's been itching to share his masterpiece prank with anyone who'll watch.

Even more than the tape, Jared braces for what's next, a tired joke that was never funny to begin with. A running gag at his expense, and he's sick of it.

"Besides, I heard you were gay now anyway," Frisco teases.

There it is. Edge sharpens Jared's voice. "Ha, ha, very funny. Just because I like to act, can dance, dress well, and *am* good-looking..."

"Whoa, relax. I was just messing with you... faggot."

Heat floods Jared's face. Without thinking, he punches Frisco's arm hard enough to shake the beaded jewelry across his neck.

The unexpected impact makes Frisco yank the steering wheel, and the vehicle swerves as the boys tense up.

Frisco regains control right before sideswiping a parked car and slams on the brakes. A tingling sensation runs down their arms as they share a wide-eyed look, then erupt into laughter.

Joseph's face scrunches with disgust as he rummages through the garbage. His frantic hunt for the napkin ramps up, fingers clawing through the mess, desperate to unearth the contact information.

"I can't find it, Mom."

Pausing to gather himself, he sits, then sags his head against the cold tile of the kitchen floor.

The shrill ring of the telephone pierces the silence, snagging his focus. *Maybe it's Bella*, he thinks, a new hope lifting his chin.

He pops up to answer. "Hello... No, no, I didn't... get out!"

Joseph's sharpness reaches Angie's ear, and she arches an eyebrow, questioning.

"Who is that? I'm not here," she whispers.

Joseph waves her off. "It's for me, alright?"

His mouth tightens, jaw locked as he resumes. "What was that? I couldn't hear the last part... Yeah, let me check."

He turns to his mother. "Ma, are you guys using the car this weekend?"

Angie shakes her head. "No, but your brother beat you to it. Daddy may be getting the van back from the shop before then."

Joseph's nose wrinkles, his lip curling into a frown. "Yeah, I can. I'll see you later," he finishes, slamming the phone down.

He despises that van. It broke down on him once, and driving it is far from comfortable. Plus, it isn't exactly a showstopper. Parked amidst a sea of Mercedes-Benzes and

BMWs dotting the island, it stands out like a tall weed in a well-manicured lawn. In contrast, the family's Altima, though not luxurious, offers a smoother ride and a more respectable look.

"You know, I don't get it. He uses that thing every night!"

One more deed Lucas does to get under his skin. His brother hasn't been shy about showing Joseph how much his return burdens Lucas and the rest of them. Joseph wonders if he's even considered the older sibling these days. After all, this was the roof he grew up under; this was supposed to be his house as well. A home where the three of them shared a bedroom, a place where they used to feel connected. An unspoken pact only brothers understand. Their mutual history all but replaced by stress and resentment.

Lucas is purposely keeping him at arm's length. "He doesn't even sleep in the room anymore; he just knocks out in the basement. What the hell is his problem? He can take the crappy van."

Angie, worn out by her boys' bickering this week, hits her wall. "Joseph, I don't want to hear it anymore."

"I'm taking that car this weekend."

"Why don't you *just* leave me alone?" she snaps, her patience on empty.

Joseph mutters under his breath, "Fine, whatever."

"Lady, I just feel like
I won't get you out of my mind
I feel love for the first time
And I know that it's true,
I can tell by the look in your eyes"
– Modjo

THREE

LADY (HEAR ME TONIGHT)

The warm rays of the sun envelope the neighborhood, spilling a golden glow on newly trimmed lawns and colorful flower beds. The tranquility is accompanied by the melodious chirps of far-off birds. Jacquelyn Castillo, a.k.a. Jackie, a.k.a. Jack-Ass, sits on the concrete stoop outside her mother's house, eagerly awaiting her boyfriend, Anthony.

The Castillo family is the Brady Bunch inverse of the Vitaglianos, with Jackie as the youngest, matching Anthony. She has three older siblings: sisters Jennie and Jamie, around Joseph and Lucas's ages, and her eldest brother, Jay, about Bella's age.

Where the families differ, however, is in the parenting. Jackie's mother, Connie, raised her four children single-handedly since divorcing Jay Sr. when Jackie was an infant. Though Jay Sr. remains involved, it's Connie who builds the daily foundation of their home.

Jackie is certain she loves Anthony with her entire sixteen-year-old being. The frost-tipped boys adorning her posters pale in comparison to his killer grin and stunning face. From the moment she caught his crystal blue stare, she knew it was game over. Even the fact that he's a year younger than her doesn't bother her in the slightest. After all, age is but a number, and he's the perfect fit, the missing meatball to her sauce. The only doubt popping up over and over again is whether he feels the same. They haven't exchanged vows or anything, but they're together now as a real-deal boyfriend and girlfriend. No one can question that she is his and he is hers, so for now, that will have to be enough.

Her heart flutters at the familiar sound of the Vitagliano's Nissan. Lucas hastily pulls up to the curb, gravel spitting as he stops. He glances at Jackie, thinking of her like a little lost puppy. He hopes Anthony's having fun at least, because he can't see their relationship lasting long. At their age, *hell, even at his own age*, getting committed isn't worth it; a lesson he's learned all too well.

With no time to dwell and no patience to stay parked, Lucas dumps Anthony off like unwanted cargo. He screeches the tires and speeds off in a cloud of dust.

Unfazed, Jackie approaches her man, greeting him with a tight embrace. Their eyes lock, their connection undeniable. They lean in for a kiss, their lips meeting in a sugary moment of teenage bliss. The bright sunshine wraps around Anthony, highlighting his casual yet stylish outfit. His hair perfectly tousled, a warm smile illuminating his face. In his presence, the air around Jackie tingles with excitement.

Inside Jackie's living room, the afternoon sunlight spills through the sheers hugging the décor in orange. Connie takes pride in keeping an immaculate house, and the room exudes a sense of comfort and familiarity. Adorned with framed photographs capturing smiling faces, every corner of the home holds a piece of her soul.

As Jackie and Anthony enter, their teenage energy brings the space to life. It's a rare shot at having the house to themselves. Connie's at work, styling the women of Staten Island's hair, while Jay moved to an apartment a year ago, and her sisters are down at the Jersey Shore, indulging in adventures of their own.

"So, what do you want to do?" Anthony asks, jumping down the foyer step.

His eyes fix on a collection of movies aligned on a nearby shelf, itching to be played. Jackie pauses, her gaze sweeping across the cozy couch, the big-screen television, the vintage record player, and the stairs leading up to the bedrooms. A sly grin dances on her lips.

"I don't know," she replies, her eyes angling toward the staircase. "We could watch a movie and cuddle up on the couch, or we could *go up to my room* and listen to some music."

Anthony can't stomach hearing the boy bands singing about being larger than life or which way they want it. He knows their dimpled faces and shiny dyed hair would be staring down at him from Jackie's walls, and he isn't in the mood to compete. It isn't that he's a hater, because honestly, Justin Timberlake's the man, but he wants to keep all of Jackie's attention on him.

Anthony is beginning to feel a deep connection with her. He knows he's attractive; girls and even women often say so. He hasn't been in the make-out game long, but in that short time, he's racked up an impressive number of conquests. However, none of that matters now that Jackie's in his life. He no longer cares about the numbers game or how effective his charms are. All he wants is to be with her, to make her happy, even if he isn't exactly sure what that means.

She sees him as himself, not as a baby or a little boy. She listens to him, shares in his ideas, and really gets him.

Anthony's tired of not being heard at home, particularly by Lucas.

When Joseph and Stella were gone, they were the only two left in the house. They've been each other's companions since Anthony was ten, and they're supposed to be close. But now there's a rift; Lucas is distant, angry, and their bond feels weak, especially with Joseph back. However, Anthony isn't concerned about that anymore. He's found someone in Jackie who makes him feel solid, like a grown-up.

Cuddling with his girl on the couch sounds like the perfect way to kick things off. "Let's start with a movie and see where the day takes us," Anthony suggests, grabbing a Jean-Claude Van Damme masterpiece off the rack.

Jackie smiles with a sigh. It's not exactly what she had in mind, but there's plenty of time for that. Time with him in her room will have to wait for another day. They settle in on the couch, content in each other's company. She's not going anywhere, and her pulse throbs knowing she remains his, and he remains hers.

They snuggle on the couch, absorbed in the movie. Van Damme's perfect splits and kicks dance across her television screen, his accented dialogue entertaining the young couple.

The outside world fades away as they laugh at the over-the-top action, playfully wrestle, and share popcorn between stolen kisses. The afternoon stretches on, hours slipping by.

They doze off, oblivious to the explosive finale. The credits roll, the soundtrack blending with their soft snores. As the sun lowers, the light flooding the room gets darker, a perfect blanket for their summertime nap.

After a long day of listening to nonstop salon gossip, thick as low-lying fog, Connie drops her guard in her still house.

She tosses her keys onto a nearby table. On the couch, she sees her daughter and her boyfriend huddled together, fast asleep, their relationship still fresh. She can't help but smile at the heartwarming image of young love, cherishing the innocence like a painting in a gallery.

This is her last child, her baby. Connie's been through the highs and crashes, the mess of heartbreaks, first with her son, then her daughters. It's been easier with Jay, she thinks. It could be the expectations placed on boys versus girls, but her daughters' emotions are a different challenge. *It started rocky but has gotten easier with time.* Now, with her youngest navigating through the trials of the heart, Connie feels like a seasoned pro, ready for the storms ahead.

Two things work in her favor. First, she genuinely likes Anthony. He's a decent kid from a solid family, easygoing around adults, not shy or *punky* like some boys she's met. Unlike them, where she forced a smile to avoid offending her daughter, Anthony's a relief.

Second, she brought home pizza, and nothing quells the teenage soul like a slice from Denino's.

"Pizza's here," Connie announces, stirring Anthony awake.

He sits up in a rush, his face turning pink as he realizes how he's pressing against her daughter.

Connie notices the blush on his cheeks but doesn't acknowledge it. She interprets his quick movements as a sign of good faith, appreciating his respect.

The two of them sit together, letting Jackie rest and enjoy an early dinner of mozzarella, crust, and sauce.

Minutes slip by as Connie asks Anthony about his summer, and he asks her what it's like to have a son surviving on his own. To an outsider, their bond could be mistaken for blood.

An hour passes, and Jackie stirs. Her eyes drift to the table, spotting the pizza box.

"Oh, pizza! When did it get here?" she asks.

Tony chuckles, "About an hour ago. You were too busy sleeping."

Jackie frowns, shooting him a look. "You didn't save me any?"

"Check the fridge," Anthony suggests.

She kicks herself for doubting them and opens the fridge, finding nothing.

"There's no pizza in here."

Anthony and Connie crack up at the look on her face.

"Who said anything about pizza? I just said, check the fridge," Anthony jabs.

Connie, unable to bear her baby's sour face, comes clean. "It's in the stove, Jackie."

Oh great, now my boyfriend has my mother playing games on me. Whose side is she on? This better not be another trick, Jackie thinks. She pulls open the oven door slowly, and there, on a baking tray, the remaining slices wait for her.

Jackie laughs at herself, relieved that they're warm, and takes them to the table. She bites into the gooey goodness, humming in delight. It's sort of cool that her boyfriend and her mother get along so well. It's kind of alright, actually. Maybe it can stay like this forever.

In the basement of his parents' house, Joseph slouches on a beat-up couch, scruffy in a plain white tank splotched with old food and sweat.

The walls gleam with the Vitagliano clan's victories. Shelves sag under a multitude of arranged trophies, plaques, ribbons, and medals. Some belong to Joseph, mostly track medals from high school, but the majority belong to Lucas, his collection still growing with recent wins.

The TV's light flickers across his tired face as the telephone rings. He glances at it, but the distance between the couch and the wall feels like a trek. The ringing dies, and moments later, his mother's muffled voice calls from upstairs.

He hears "Joseph," "brother," and "Jackie's," but the rest is incoherent, like the muffled teachers from Charlie Brown.

Joseph grumbles, drags himself off the couch, and shuffles upstairs.

"I need you to pick your brother up from Jackie's," Angie says, no question in her tone.

This is new; he assumed Lucas, having the car, left him stranded. "Can't Lucas pick him up on his way home?" Joseph pleads.

"No, he already left."

Joseph peers out the living room window. "Ma, what are you talking about? The car's in the driveway."

"Yeah, so go pick up Anthony." She huffs.

Joseph, exasperated with Lucas for hogging the car every chance he gets, yet never helping, presses. "Why can't Lucas do it? He's been using the car all day."

"I told you he's not here; his friends grabbed him a little while ago," Angie snaps. *It's always this way,* she thinks. She asks one son to do something, and they demand why the other one can't. Just once, she'd love to have something done without a song and dance.

Joseph could've done something today, perhaps gone somewhere, if not for Lucas. He didn't even know the car was back. The least Lucas could've done was say he wasn't using it. Not that Joseph has grand plans, or any plans, or even people to see, but having the option would've been considerate.

He grits his teeth, realizing it's late and someone has to get Anthony.

Angie watches him grab a jacket and slide on house slippers. "You're not going out *like that?*"

Joseph glances down at himself, the smiling face boxers grinning up at him. "Yep, I am."

He kicks the door open and calls for the keys.

"They're on the stairs." Angie's squint betraying disgust. All these years, she kept her sons sharp, hair combed, shirts ironed, and pants worn when exiting the house.

Joseph snags the keys, jingles them with a teasing grin, laughs at her expression, and steps into the night.

"And now he's home and we're laughing
Like we always did
My same old, same old friend
Until a quarter to ten, I saw the strain creep in
He seems distracted
And I know just what is gonna happen next
Before his first step, He is off again."
-Pearl Jam

Four

OFF HE GOES

Joseph slowly wakes up and blearily scans the room. The remnants of a wild dream about missed homework, threatening graduation, fade from his cracked eyelids.

He reaches for the nearby alarm clock and winces at the glaring numbers: one in the afternoon. The alarm didn't go off, or he slept through it, or maybe he forgot to set it. It doesn't matter now; the day's half gone, and dwelling on it won't help. He has exciting plans. *Today is the day I'm going to get back on the starting line.*

The last few months at college were a whirlwind, full of graduation excitement, speech prep, final exams with a capital F, and soaking up every possible second with his girl. By contrast, the past two weeks in Staten Island felt hollow, directionless.

Recognizing the rut he's fallen into, Newton's first law drifts into his mind: an object in motion tends to stay in motion, while an object at rest tends to stay at rest. Right now, Joseph's rooted in the "at rest" category.

A grainy flashback flickers: his high school self, straining against the wind, arms and legs pumping, stalking the runner in front of him, determined to pass. That fire still lingers, faint but real.

He needs to grab that fire again. Joseph swings his legs over the mattress and gears up for a run. It's been four years since he last trained, but as he pulls on a tank top, shorts, and laces his sneakers, the familiar competitor's rush surges through him.

With Lucas gone, there'd be no smart remarks to dodge, and Joseph anticipates a critique-free day. Anthony's lost in an AIM chatroom, his parents are running errands, and the house is quiet for once, a welcome change. Joseph's sure no interruptions are coming.

Stepping onto Sinclair Ave, Joseph is met by a stunning summer day. The sky, a sharp blue, is dotted with cotton-candy clouds floating overhead. Yellow and pink flowers dance in a mild breeze. He can hear the leaves rustling, and the scent of fresh-cut grass tickles his nostrils. It's the perfect day for a restart.

He knows the first run back will test him. It's important to start slow. His muscles have softened over the years, and despite his experience, he'll need to treat his legs as if starting new.

Head high, shoulders squared, he feels ready. The first stride drops off the small stoop of his parents' house onto the winding concrete path to the sidewalk. He keeps his pace restrained, a touch faster than walking, but not quite a jog. No need to push too hard. Each stride builds confidence; he covers the 60-foot stretch to the sidewalk with ease. His feet land on the pavement rhythmically, each stride covering more and more ground.

Houses streak past as he picks up speed. Instinct takes over, propelling him beyond his limits, chasing that old medal high. He's wired to train at a varsity level; he runs to compete, he runs to win.

But his body fights back, and the strain builds fast. Joseph fights to dial back the urge to push, his old habits colliding with his current state. He would have to unlearn what he has learned. His lungs hitch, burning with each breath. The medals hanging in the basement feel like they belong to a stranger, some phantom of the starting line, only existing in the past.

Joseph reaches the end of the block and the end of his run.

Cars zip by the intersection of Sinclair and Foster, drivers casting sidelong glances. Joseph, gut spilling over his tank top, shorts clinging tightly, feels exposed, small.

Defeat weighs heavy. His head sinks below slumping shoulders as he turns and trudges the seventy yards back to his parents' house.

Descending into the basement, Joseph plops down onto the beat-up old couch and scans the silent room for something else to do. *Perhaps tomorrow could be a better day for running.* He grabs a controller, swaps the wrestling cartridge in his Nintendo 64 for something more his speed, and settles in. The John Williams theme blares as yellow letters scroll up the screen.

Firming his position, Joseph braces for a marathon session. It's time to fire up his trusty X-wing and take down the Galactic Empire. At least this is something he can do today; no need to dwell on past glories when a galaxy needs saving.

He virtually pilots his spacecraft for hours, red lasers blasting screeching Tie Fighters. His attack run zeroes in on the enemy's shield generators, *almost there*, a few more shots to hard-fought glory. The telephone rings. "Stay on target," he mutters, ignoring it. This is important work; he has one life left, it's the last level, and the Emperor's waiting.

But the ringing won't quit, and it shatters his zen-like focus. His thumbs blur over the controller, synced with every shot. He's one with the Force. Feeling its mystical energies, his Jedi pilot dodges the squealing green lasers. On the twentieth ring, a stray blast rips through his deflector shields, exploding his starship into a million pixels of space dust. The Empire's reign endures, crushing the galaxy under its heel.

Joseph hurls the controller; it clatters against the tile. Jaw tight, he succumbs and drags himself up for the grudging five-foot trek to the phone.

"Hello?" His posture straightens. "Ezra, hey, what's up?" Ezra's voice feels like a lifeline.

To Joseph, Ezra is the closest thing to family without being actual family. They met as sixth-grade rivals, became high school teammates, and by nineteen, Joseph stood next to Ezra as his best man.

Their history is a wild ride. Ezra marrying first and having a kid still blows his mind. Trouble followed Ezra like a shadow. He'd often drag them into tight spots, leaving them to scramble, but none was bigger than the night of Black Tuesday.

Ezra, Joseph, and two of their teammates went to a private party at some girl's place, Ezra, of course, leading them there, dead-set on hooking up. While he disappeared with her, doing what teenage boys do, Joseph and the rest of the crew hung out with her uninterested friends. Booze flowed, loosening tongues, easing the awkwardness enough. Flirting followed, and on the cusp of the discomfort turning into actual fun, her boyfriend showed up.

His unexpected entrance, backed by a much larger gang, killed the whole mood. Ezra and the boys bolted out of the apartment and ended up down the block near a gas station. After begging the attendant to use the phone, Joseph dialed home right as the boyfriend and his gang rolled up. The attendant, wanting no part of it, shoved the group outside to face them. Knowing they were about to get jumped, Joseph grabbed an empty beer bottle off the ground. The boyfriend charged; Ezra dropped him fast, possibly breaking his nose. Ezra locked in, his fists continuing despite the kid going limp. As the gang closed in, Joseph Sr. pulled up.

Joseph Sr., like a pissed-off bouncer, bulldozed his way through the crowd. He grabbed the boys, threw them in his car, and sniffed the air. He ripped into them for the alcohol on their breaths and peeled out.

Once home, he sat them down at the kitchen table, and despite their protests, called each of their parents.

As the boys protested, Joseph Sr. reached into his waistband and slammed a pistol on the table. The gun hit the table with a sharp crack, silencing their excuses. Ezra's toughness melted into tears. No one was smiling that night, especially as each parent filed in to recover their sons, but by the next day it became legend and many a laugh was shared over it.

Their teen years weren't all chaos; they were filled with keg parties, fly girls in crop tops, track meets throughout the city, dark theaters next to pretty ladies, long talks about life, clubbing with hot chicks, lazy summer nights enjoying Boyz II Men, and of course, cruising the Island for all the honeys.

They would call dibs on who they wanted, and being mindful of the guy code, those calls were mostly respect-ed. It helped that they were naturally attracted to varying styles, making them excellently paired wingmen for each other.

Joseph, with his deep brown eyes, reeled them in with his dimpled smile, and Ezra hooked them with his charm. He had the gift, knowing all the right things to say to keep them interested.

Now, years later, Joseph leans into the phone. "No, nothing much, just hanging around," he says, voice hesitant.

Pumped to hear Ezra at first, he fumbles for words, searching for anything to talk about, grasping for their old rhythm.

"Yeah, sure." He twists the cord, "I started running again, too." The half-truth bites.

"What time? Alright, cool. I'll see you then." He hangs up. *Did Ezra catch the awkwardness? Nah, just overthinking it.* "This will be good," he tells himself. "Once we're together, we'll find the same pace, and it'll be like it was."

With the call done, Joseph grabs fresh laundry from his mom's dryer and heads upstairs. He cranks the radio, performs a little dance in the mirror, and changes his clothes.

The woody scent of Aqua Di Giò cologne and sweat fills Joseph's nose as he turns the key. The van coughs to life, patched up enough to roll but still handling like a barge; sluggish, with no kick when he floors it. It chugs down the streets like a rickety cart, but at least the CD player still works.

Joseph built a hefty music collection, a majority from those "ten CDs for a penny" scams where he'd forget to mail back the overpriced extras. He pulls out his bulging binder, plastic sleeves crackling as he flips to a worn page. The CDs are arranged with precision: alphabetical by artist, then release year. Pop, rap, techno, and R&B - no country music in sight.

Alternative rock reigns, with Pearl Jam leading the pack. Introduced when a high school crush gifted him a Pearl Jam tee for his birthday, his obsession really took off during his college years. The poetic lyrics and raw emotion flowing from Eddie and his bandmates surpassed Prince's funky chords as his new favorite. He'd haunt Where House Records in East Lansing, diligently searching for rarer and rarer recordings, and he'd pore over bootlegs and concert releases. Hunting variant releases of the same track, snagging every single to discover B-sides not found on the albums. Eddie's gravelly croon weaving through jagged riffs stuck to Joseph like distressed flannel.

As "Yellow Ledbetter" strums its last echo, the van rattles up to Ezra's house.

The driver's side door groans as Joseph slides out, pocketing his keys. He looks up and finds the front door open. Ezra, backlit against the entryway, stands waiting for him, a freshly trimmed goatee outlining his jawline, his thick, wavy hair slicked tight with gel. Like Joseph, he's broader since varsity days, but his dark Indo-Brazilian features remain handsome.

"Hey, good to see you, man. Come on in," Ezra calls, flashing a toothy grin with arms outstretched.

Joseph exhales, the tension slipping from his shoulders as he advances into the house. *Man, it feels exciting to be out.* He pulls Ezra into a hug, holding on a moment longer than usual.

Ezra, Jessica, and their two-year-old son Donnie squeeze into his in-laws' place, their family space a little room upstairs. Jessica grew up here, a grade below them, right down the block from Ezra. She wasn't part of his grand plan, the convenient girl next door, an easy hookup. The lovesick neighbor conveniently placed so Ezra could prowl for more. Their path to family was a mess of detours: boy meets girl, boy hooks up with girl, boy dumps girl, boy sees her at a club with some guy, boy beats up guy, boy leaves with girl, boy spots another girl, boy dumps girl again, girl beats up new girl, and around and around the big-top show of their relationship went. Looking back, it's obvious it was only ever going to be those two in the end, but when you're inside the storm, it's harder to see the patterns emerge.

Jessica became his constant. Maybe it was because they lived close, or perhaps they always had a deeper connection that Joseph missed. Whatever the case, Jessica became one of the crew.

She pecks Joseph's cheek, and he takes her in. Still the same girl from high school, her dark curly hair bouncing, her face too young to be someone's mother. She excuses herself and slips upstairs, giving them space. They settle in the living room, a new experience for Joseph. Past visits were quick dashes to the basement, hiding beer breath from her parents, Jessica setting him up with friends so she and Ezra could fool around. Nights ended sprawled on ripped couches amid '80s knick-knacks and dust-covered paperbacks.

Ezra mentions the in-laws are out, then ducks to the kitchen. "I'm grabbing a beer; you want something?"

Joseph glances at the door, then at Ezra. He holds off on the drink. They'd kept plans vague; he hesitates. "Nah, I'm alright."

He scans the living room. Same fringed lamps on top of the same scuffed tables, next to the same floral couch; frozen in time. A TiVo box and framed photos of Ezra, Jessica, and Donnie are the only noticeable updates.

"Nothing? I got soda, beer?" Ezra nudges.

Joseph spots Donnie's baby photo, a perfect clone of his father, and realizes tonight's going to be a chill one. Fine with him either way. Joseph doesn't even know where to find a good time on the Island anymore, and driving into the city sounds like a hassle, not a thrill.

"Sure, grab me whatever you're having then," he says, settling into the couch.

It's tight, Ezra, juggling the house with the in-laws, but he's making it work. Joseph's dimple pops from a smirk. Ezra's got this.

As they talk, his eyes linger on Donnie's picture. *How's Ezra a dad?* Over two years since that panicked confession in the car. A kid fathering a kid, his face etched with fear and defeat. Ezra's mom lost to cancer a few months after high school, his scholarship shattered by a blown-out knee, his dreams crumbling. Finding out he was going to be a father was supposed to bring tears of joy, not sobs of desperation.

Joseph's memories drift through Ezra's recent storms. Panic, tears, dropping out to scrape by; fatherhood hit like a tempest, yet he stands, a family man.

Married, kid, family. Joseph pictures Bella here, post-grad, beside him. Could it be like this for them? The couch creaks as he shifts, the thought a quiet pang.

Ezra hands him a Red Wolf; they tap the bottles and twist the caps.

"I've been with Bella for over two years now," Joseph says.

"Oh yeah, how is that? You never stay with people that long," Ezra takes a swig.

"Yeah, she's great," Joseph's mind drifts forward.

He takes a long drag from his bottle, then fixes Ezra with a curious look. "What have you been doing? What have you been up to? You ever go out?"

Ezra chokes on his beer, spilling some, laughing out the rest. "Don't really get out much, not really." He wipes his sleeve across the mess. "Sometimes play cards at my sister's. Cool bunch of guys, you'd like them, arrogant like us."

Joseph laughs as Donnie storms in. A whirlwind of chaotic energy only a two-year-old can unleash, and he wraps his small arms around his father. Joseph's caught off guard; the boy had shot up since he last saw him.

"Oh my god, I didn't realize how long it's been. He got so big! Hey Donnie, what's going on?" Joseph holds up his hand for a high-five.

Donnie squints at the strange man in his house and leaves him hanging. No high-five for you. He clings to his daddy tighter, leans into Ezra's ear, and whispers.

Ezra stares into his son's eyes and taps him on the nose. "Alright, alright, hey, go tell mommy, okay?"

Joseph watches, awed, as Ezra Jedi mind-tricks his son away. He grins. The old Ezra would've barked orders, not tapped noses.

"What did he say?" Joseph asks.

Ezra shrugs. "I don't know." They burst out in laughter.

Donnie's arrival cracks the dam, and they talk for a long time.; Joseph about his last year leading up to graduation, and Ezra on the challenges of changing diapers and early morning wake-ups.

As the evening winds down, the men bid their farewells at the front of the house.

"It was good to see you. You should come play cards with us sometime," Ezra offers.

"I will, I will," Joseph says, half-committed but grateful for the invitation.

With one last hug, Ezra lets him go. Joseph heads to the van, pausing for a moment to watch the front door close. Tonight isn't what he thought it would be. Joseph sits in the van, staring at the house. *This feels like a long goodbye, not a reunion.*

He starts the engine, time and change pressing down on him like a weighted blanket. Ezra's hurdles flash before him: his mom, the pregnancy, postponing college, and becoming a family man. His friend was forced to figure things out on his own.

Joseph pictured storming in, a knight to lift his friend from ruin. But Ezra's fine now, thriving in a world he no longer fits into. Joseph rubs his eyes, wipes the dryness from his lips, and drives away. Eddie's voice rises through the speakers, the road unfurling as he glances in the rearview mirror. The porch light dims, a fragment of the past slipping into shadow.

The sky stretches out, morning clouds filtering the sunlight and casting a pale blue haze over distant bridges and cluttered rooftops. The van pulls up beside a row of gravestones, coming to a slow stop on the crunchy gravel roadway. Joseph hops out. His footsteps lead him down a path he'd traveled only once before, yet the route remains vivid in his mind. It's a short distance to the stone he's looking for.

Kneeling in front of the gray marble marker, he studies his grandfather's etched face, forever smiling. The air carries the faint scent of damp earth, grounding him in the moment.

"Hi, Grandpa. I hope everything's well for you, wherever you are," Joseph says, then pauses. "I don't know where I am anymore, who I am anymore... You missed so much, so much. I miss you. Everything's just so different; everything is just so not right..."

The words catch in his throat, too frail for the weight in his chest. He sighs and brushes the dirt from the etched letters. Slapping the sides of his legs to clean them, Joseph leans down, places his hand on the gravestone, and traces his grandfather's name.

"Joseph Vitagliano, your name, my name."

"You don't even know me
You say that I'm not living right
You don't understand me
So why do you judge my life?"
- Armand Van Helden

FIVE

YOU DON'T KNOW ME

As summer days fly past, the number of knuckle-heads crowding the Vitagliano's basement swells. Lucas, Anthony, Jared, and Frisco, sprawled across the couch like permanent fixtures, are joined by two more of Lucas's buddies: Hatcher, a stocky, muscled paisan, and Donnie, a wiry Irish kid who'd been tearing up the block since they were kids.

Sinclair Avenue had always been a boys' block, a place where childhood memories were forged first on Big Wheels and later with tricked-out Mongoose bikes. The boys would race through the backyards, a wild pack darting between houses before fences and above-ground pools tamed the landscape. There was Frankie Four Eyes, always squinting through those thick lenses, and Richie the Bum, a Puerto Rican kid whose bike tricks left the rest of them jealous. Down at the corner across from the wooded lot lived Matt the Mistake, whose siblings were a decade older and long gone. Ethan and Eric, two houses down, were identical twins inseparable as shadows, while Fuji, real name Bobby, lived across the street with a father who looked eerily like Saddam Hussein. The older kids, Dave and Chris, leaned hard into metal over freestyle music, sneaking out whenever they could, their dad glaring from behind the blinds, convinced Nintendo was a Japanese plot to brainwash America's youth.

One face Joseph couldn't help missing these days was Vic Maritino, a sweet, fair-haired kid who'd made the Vitagliano basement his second home back in the day. Vic and Lucas were like peanut butter and jelly, always stuck together, sharing every free minute. His absence now felt strange, given their history on the Avenue. Instead, only Donnie remains, still hanging around as the last native of the block in the basement.

But those days were long gone. Now, beside an empty pizza box littered with chicken wing bones and oily napkins, the crew was lost in digital pro-wrestling combat. Fingers crunch buttons, joysticks flicking in a mad four-player free-for-all. Lucas picks his blocky digital avatar, the skeleton-clad Lucha-dor, La Parka. Frisco mains the all-powerful Goldberg.

"I'm sure! I'm sure La Parka just tossed Goldberg!" Frisco yells, knuckles white, as his top-tier character gets rag-dolled by a lowlife jobber.

"Viva La Parka!" Lucas crows, hoisting his controller like a champ.

"Yeah, it's real hard to run around in circles. You are so cheap," Donnie scoffs, rolling his eyes at Lucas' in-ring strategy.

Lucas shrugs, voice cracking mid-taunt. "What's the matter? I'm too good? Viva La Parka!"

Joseph slips downstairs unnoticed, soaking in the scene. Their easy banter, laced with sarcasm and packed with horrible insults, draws a marveling stare. Laughter bounces off the walls in lieu of anger. He leans against the stairwell, a tightness creeping into his chest, envy sharp as a blade as he watches their effortless vibe and thinks of his own far-away friends.

"What the hell are you guys doing?" he calls from the steps.

Anthony, rooting for Donnie's downfall and itching for his turn, answers, "NWO Revenge Tournament. I got next."

"Well, I just had Donnie's mom," Lucas trash-talks, maneuvering his wrestler around in circles, dodging the grapples of his polygonal rivals.

"Oh, so funny," Donnie deadpans, smiling.

"No, seriously," Lucas presses, "Don't worry. She's good. Right, Frisco?"

Frisco claps his hands. "No complaints."

"Well, I can understand that, considering I just had Frisco's mom," Donnie fires back.

Frisco mashes the multicolored buttons, and Goldberg executes a jackhammer, slamming his opponent headfirst into the mat. The furious on-screen action splits his focus. He scrambles for a comeback but comes up empty. He's got nothing for Donnie.

Spotting his opening, Anthony pounces. "Yeah, but Frisco's mom being a slut is old news. Your mom is actually good in bed." Frisco winces; Donnie flushes, an effective one-two punch. Hatcher guffaws, and Jared flashes Anthony a thumbs-up. "Good one," he adds.

"Yep, my mom's a slut, but yours is..." Frisco trails off as Goldberg pins Donnie's avatar, Scott Hall. The ref counts one, the ref counts two, the ref counts three. Victory. A satisfying end, actions achieving what his words didn't. Frisco leaps up, flexing and pointing for an imaginary crowd.

He hovers over Donnie and poses down on top of him. Donnie stands, scowling. "Alright, already. Enough. I'm going home."

The boys erupt, pouncing like piranhas on fresh meat. "Come on now, don't be like that. Relax. Take it easy," Jared teases. "You know, like your mother."

Donnie's grin sharpens. "That's it! You know it's time to leave when the fag starts talking about screwing your mother." He hurls a pillow at Jared's head, giggling so hard he can barely breathe.

"I am not a fag!" Jared protests.

Donnie slaps his hands as if removing chalk and points finger guns at Jared. "Sure, you're not a homosexual," he mocks in an Eddie Murphy voice, then struts past Joseph.

"Don't leave. Come on, we're just joking, joking," Lucas laughs. Donnie turns around and, with a smile, gives the room a double middle-finger salute.

"Please, with the abuse I take, you guys never stop making fun of my mother," Frisco adds.

It's true. Frisco and his mom took the brunt of the guys' ribbing, with mentions of her a constant punchline. Donnie, on the other hand, didn't care how well he could handle it. He's an Irish boy, and stereotype or not, he will not abide anyone talking foul about his mom. Donnie twirls both hands, concluding his salute. Then leaves.

"He's really mad, huh?" Joseph asks, making his way to the couch.

"Nah, he does that all the time," Anthony says, snagging the abandoned controller. "I'm next!" The group continues like nothing's changed; it was just Donnie being Donnie.

Joseph sinks onto the couch beside Hatcher. "Hey, how are you and your girl?" Hatcher asks.

"Great," Joseph says, keeping it casual despite the ache. "I miss her, you know, but we're good." He met the kid a short time ago but can't stop oversharing. "We plan to talk at least once a week, and we email all the time."

"Oh, Joe, Bella called earlier," Anthony says, eyes locked on Scott Hall's pyro-heavy entrance.

"And I talked to her yesterday," Lucas cuts in, running La Parka around the ring.

"Did she leave her new number?" Joseph asks.

Lucas and Anthony chorus, "Yeah, but I didn't write it down."

Lifting his voice over the TV, Joseph says, "Good thing she emailed it to me earlier this week."

He's learned the hard way, after rummaging through the trash once already, not to trust his brothers with matters of his heart. He grits his teeth, watching them shrug off Bella's call like it's nothing. *Don't they care?*

Lucas is persistently surrounded by his crew, and Anthony's glued to Jackie; they know what it is to need other people. So, where's the compassion for their own brother? *How can they not get it?*

"Hey, hey, where's the tape?" Frisco shouts, diving into a pile of VHS cassettes.

Jared's eyes snap to Frisco, his posture stiffening. "I've got to get going."

"What tape?" Joseph asks.

"The wildlife video," Frisco mutters.

Joseph scrunches his face. *Wildlife video?*

Jared adds a kick of bass to his voice, "I'm leaving."

"Oh, where are you going?" Frisco calls as Jared bolts.

"I have to go. Lou, I'll call you later," Jared says, ignoring him.

"All right, catch you later," Lucas replies.

Hatcher nudges Joseph's shoulder, "You've never seen this; it's ridiculous. Insane!"

Joseph wonders what's on this tape. Clearly, Jared's unease and the group's excitement hint at something epic. Frisco raises his rectangular prize, triumphant.

"Here it is! Now just watch," Frisco exclaims, popping the coveted tape into the VCR.

Frisco changes the input on the television, and the screen buzzes alive with digital snow fading into grainy footage. Frisco kills the lights, allowing the TV's pale glow to take over.

On screen, Frisco, Lucas, Anthony, and Hatcher appear, draped in all black, like some sort of K-Mart ninjas, their faces smeared with dark makeup.

Beneath a black-knit cap, Frisco's eyes glint as he stabilizes the camera. As the boys exit the frame, a new world emerges behind them. The focus shifts to a tranquil road, shrouded in darkness. A dim streetlight spills an eerie color over the scene. Joseph can make out a few trees in the surrounding woods and an old, decaying telephone pole. In the frame, the four young men stare at the pole, their attention centered on its lone occupant, a reflective yellow sign with the silhouette of a black horse.

In the basement, Frisco can't stay still, hopping near the television like a carnival barker. "We needed to get that sign!" He narrates. His tone, usually thick with humor and snark, belies an intensity that is entirely novel to Joseph's ears.

Joseph sees no ladder or apparent means for the boys to reach the sign. Taking it down is illegal, so he's clearly watching criminal genius unfold. On the tape, Anthony climbs onto Hatcher's shoulders, wobbling as he reaches out for the sign. Joseph snorts, clutching his sides as he watches them fumble. *It's like The Great Muppet Caper; only question, which one is Gonzo?*

"We had to borrow your mother's makeup for the camouflage," Frisco adds.

"Some of the clothes are mommy's too; we couldn't find enough black," Anthony shares, laughing.

Joseph studies the screen and sure enough spots Anthony rocking a woman's blouse. Before he can ask why they'd attempt this, other than what he assumes to be boredom, the camera jerks, cutting to a new angle. On screen, Lucas sprints and leaps, his body colliding with the metal sign. The crash rings out like a cheap drum, but the sign doesn't budge. Lucas crashes hard, sprawling face-first into the mud. The boys howl.

"Yo, play that again," Hatcher cackles.

"When did you guys do this? Why did you guys do this?" Joseph asks.

Frisco's jaw tightens, his voice dropping flat. "Sometimes people need to know what they are."

The tape cuts to inside Frisco's car, their hard-won prize jammed between Anthony and Hatcher in the back. Frisco seizes the sign and darts out of the car, heading towards a nearby house.

On-screen, Frisco slinks through the darkness, hiding behind a bush, then jetting behind a tree. "Some people are animals, and some people just look like animals," Frisco continues, as he watches himself stake the sign by the front door. "And sometimes, certain girls need a keepsake to remind them exactly what kind of animal they truly are."

The tape ends with Frisco back in the car, his arm pointing at the sign with a triumphant grin, a loud-and-clear message for whoever opens the door. "Now you know you're a horse," Frisco declares, his face filling the screen before it snaps to a bright chroma blue.

Amazed, Joseph comments, "Wow, you guys must hate that girl."

Anthony shrugs. "I don't even know her."

"You don't know the half of what Frisco has put this girl through," Lucas says.

"What in God's green earth could you have possibly done to this girl?" Joseph presses.

Frisco grins, stretching his arms, ready to work. "Now, Joe, you know me. I get along with everybody... but this one, oh man." His arms come alive, gesticulating with every syllable. "She's been a thorn in my side since grade school. A constant pain in the ass, always pointing out what she doesn't like about me." He places his hands together in a prayer-like salute, shaking them toward the heavens. "One time, we were all at her house: me, your brother, Donnie, pretty much everybody. We were just hanging out, no big deal, and we started playing Truth or Dare. So she's trying to be funny all night, making fun of me, my mother, my ass, whatever."

"But only one man is the Ass Man," Lucas interjects.

Frisco's mouth drops open at the interruption. "Yes, we know you're the Ass Man," he retorts.

"That's right. You can be a Luke-ass," Joseph adds, smirking.

"Fuck off," Lucas fires back, his smile vanishing.

Joseph flinches. "Nice language. I'm just joking around. No need for that shit."

Lucas leans in, his voice sharp. "Why are you here? Whose friends are down here anyway?"

Joseph blinks, lips thinning at Lucas's sudden edge. They'd been joking around all afternoon, but now he's taking it to another level. Joseph had only responded in kind to the banter; he watches them do it repeatedly. *It isn't his fault that Lucas set himself up for an easy tease,* he thinks. But in their dynamic, it's all about who's dishing out the shit and who's swallowing it.

Frisco cuts through the noise, his voice rising. "Can I finish? Can I?" With one glance at his gathered audience, he steers them back from their petty clash. "Okay, then. Like I was saying, we were playing Truth or Dare, and Mrs. Ed started to get under my skin." He brings his hands up near his face and clenches them into tight fists, knuckles paling with tension. "So she turns and tells me, 'You've been real quiet. Why don't you ask somebody a question?'" Frisco outstretches his hand, his fingers twitching like a Fourth of July sparkler. "That was it! I turn to Donnie, 'Truth or Dare?' He says 'truth,' and I turn back to Shelley, look her straight in the eye," Frisco points into the air as if she's standing right there in the basement, his eyes bulging, "and I say, 'Donnie, who in this room looks most like a *HORSE?* Lucas doubles over, laughing."

"Right away, I got up from the table and left," Lucas adds.

"Shelley starts screaming at Donnie," Frisco mimics, "'You better not say me, or you can get fuck-all out of my house.'" Returning to his normal tone, Frisco points at Lucas. "As she's talking, I hear Lucas tripping down the stairs over his own laughter. And Donnie, he's looking back and forth between me and Shelley, desperate not to burst out laughing himself. Then he says, 'Me!' and points at himself." Frisco turns his thumbs inward, then raises one finger into the air. "But she knew. I made sure she knew right then and there; she knows she's a horse."

"Jared doesn't find it amusing. He used to date her," Hatcher informs Joseph.

Joseph tries another shot at trash-talking with the guys. "So let me get this straight: he's gay and into bestiality?"

"Everybody needs to really cut that shit out. He's not gay," Lucas declares, his smile gone.

Joseph's jaw clenches. Lucas isn't simply defending Jared; he's shoving Joseph out. Frisco raises an eyebrow. Joseph hasn't said anything about Jared; he hasn't heard Lucas say himself.

Catching Frisco's expression, Lucas adds, "I think it's really starting to bother him." He turns his head from the group and shuts off the television.

Lucas strolls down the sidewalk and turns into a development where rows of attached houses stretch ahead, their identical red panels like plastic pieces on a Monopoly board. He takes a bite of his overstuffed bagel, balancing it to keep the contents from spilling as he climbs the three small steps of Jared's stoop. He presses the doorbell and waits, chewing. Lucas watches as a couple of kids ride bicycles nearby, jumping the curbs and crossing on and off the sidewalk. The front door swings open, and behind the entryway, a small, wheelchair-bound Jewish woman in her mid-fifties invites him in.

Lucas greets Jared's mother with a kiss on the cheek and lets himself inside. The house feels stuck in another era, not like his mom's style, but still warm and welcoming. Alongside the expected tchotchkes and photographs, it's adapted for wheelchair mobility, with ample spaces and a wall-mounted chair lift for the upper floor.

"Hey, is Jared home?" Lucas asks.

"Yeah, I think he's downstairs watching TV. You know where the basement is, right?" Jared's mother replies.

Of course, Lucas knows the way; he's been coming here since he was ten. These questions are her quiet way to either spark a conversation or make sure he's comfortable. Lucas doesn't pity her; she'd have none of it anyway. Life's a crapshoot, and she rolls with it, still caring, still a mother and wife, wheelchair or not.

He nods and heads toward the stairwell. Downstairs, Jared lounges on the couch, idly flipping through various cable channels.

Boredom rolls on Jared like a spinning rainbow wheel of death. He's stuck on repeat, cycling through station after station. *57 channels? More like 157 channels with nothing on.* The massive screen his dad bolted to the wall, a testament to his handiwork, might as well be a painting. Then, a light in the darkness, the sight of California sunshine floods the canvas. Pamela Anderson, vibrant in her red swimsuit, bounces toward him on the screen, snapping him to attention.

Jared's eyes dart around the basement. The Groucho, Harpo, and Chico statuettes stare back, the only company besides his mother in the house, and she's not running down anytime soon. His face flickers between a smirk and a flush of shame. Slowly, he unzips his jeans and moves his hand toward his crotch.

As Jared relaxes into a rhythm, he hears the thump and thud of feet from the stairwell. He freezes mid-action, scrambling to adjust his clothing. He fumbles with the remote, accidentally changing the channel.

"What are you doing? Oh my God!" Lucas exclaims, catching Jared with little Jared hanging out.

Pinned by Lucas's stare, Jared forces himself to peek at the television. Pamela's no longer running on the beach; instead, the screen is filled with the sculpted physiques of an ESPN bodybuilding competition. Sculpted male bodies gleam with oil, muscles rippling under stage lights, and legs flexing in tiny Speedos.

"Bro, you *are* a fucking queer, dude," Lucas bursts out, laughing uncontrollably.

Jared opens his mouth, but only a stutter spills out as he struggles to pull up his jeans. Finally, he manages to blurt out, "I-I swear it's not what it looks like!"

Still laughing, Lucas hurls his sandwich at Jared. Lettuce and tomato explode across Jared's shirt, mayo smearing his stomach. Lucas dashes upstairs, Jared chasing after him. In his haste, Jared zips up too fast, yelping as the metal teeth clamp onto more than they should.

Shit, he's already gone. Jared hurries past his mother and out the front door, shooting past Lucas. Catching him from the corner of his eye, he spins around. Lucas is on the stoop, doubled over, hands on his knees, roaring with laughter.

"Where you going?" Lucas calls out.

Jared waits for Lucas to catch his breath. "Oh, I thought you left. Look, it wasn't what it looked like."

"I've done it enough myself to realize what it was," Lucas laughs again. "Me, I would've been watching something different," he quips, raising his eyebrows.

"That's what I wanted to let you know," Jared scrambles, afraid of the endless jokes about to come his way, especially once Donnie catches wind.

Lucas waves him off, his effort to calm Jared's nerves betrayed by the giggles spilling out. "I don't want to hear it. Be whatever you want to be. If you like guys, you like guys. Hell, we'll get into the clubs quicker."

"Jesus, I'm not like that, alright?" Jared's voice spikes, his hands flailing. "I was watching Baywatch. Bouncing women in bikinis! I don't know how ESPN came on!"

"Nice choice of words," Lucas chuckles, pointing at the wet and nasty mayo stain on Jared's stomach. His grin widens; he knows Jared hates the teasing, but fuck his feelings, this shit is funny.

Jared's eyes dart to Lucas, silently begging for mercy. The guys already bust his balls enough; honestly, how much worse could it get?

Jared fidgets. "So, what do you want to do?" he blurts, desperate to change the subject.

"I don't know, let's grab a bite to eat. I kind of lost my lunch back there," Lucas says, stifling the last giggle.

"Shit man, you threw up?" Would he really be so grossed out if I was gay? Jared wonders.

"No, when I threw my food at you, dumbass," Lucas clarifies, wiping Jared's shirt, flicking off crumbs and soggy bits of lettuce.

Lucas's beeper clangs like a tin can alarm. He glances at it, a smirk tugging at his mouth.

"Who is it?" Jared asks.

"Some girl I met last night," Lucas replies. "I'll call her later. You never know, she might even have a brother or something for you."

Jared shakes his head, a grin breaking through. Lucas's teasing finally cracks him, and he can't help but laugh. Besides, now that he's had time to think about the absurdity of what happened, he has to admit, *that shit was funny.*

"Straight from the slums of Shaolin
Wu-Tang Killa Beez on a swarm
Your soul have just been tooken
Through the 36 Chambers of death, kid"
-Wu-Tang Clan

Six

36 CHAMBERS

The blinking cursor mocks Joseph with every flash of the empty screen. He sits in the basement corner, isolated at the family computer for what feels like days. At some point, he has to secure a job, not any old employment this time, but the start of a career. This isn't some temporary gig with a built-in expiration date, like the summers he spent lifeguarding or the odd university jobs he took for beer money. This is *the big one*, the decision that will shape the rest of his life.

Up until now, there have always been goals to achieve, little pockets of celebrations close beyond the horizon: learning to walk, mastering pee-pee on the potty, stepping up from pre-K to kindergarten, graduating elementary school, surviving junior high, excelling on the SATs, and earning that college degree. Growing up was a prelude to this moment, sitting down to write the resume that will kick his life into motion. Yet, as Joseph faces the cold glow of the empty monitor, his accomplishments feel inadequate, small.

He has always strived to do his best. He hasn't always succeeded, but he believes doing the right thing is enough. He isn't rebellious like his sister was growing up, nor does he have Lucas's natural athletic talents; his brother's ease with sports leaves him lazy elsewhere. He lacks Anthony's instinctive compassion, his younger brother's ability to connect with anyone, even strangers.

Joseph is the responsible one: the kid who's been reading newspapers since he was four, who skipped a grade, who soaked up *you're so smart* comments his whole life. Praise he accepted, even when he didn't deserve it.

His Bachelor of Science in Chemistry is intended to be his ticket to greater things. He ventured far from home, left the family safety net, and earned it on his own. Yet, in the dim, musty basement, thick with the hum of the computer tower, he misses Bella. *She saw how hard he fought for it.* Now he questions if it was even worth the trouble.

Truth is, Joseph stumbled into Chemistry. He switched majors when his initial focus of study, Forensic Science, was discontinued after his freshman year. He entered Michigan State dreaming of working in a crime lab, a field offered to undergrads at only three schools: one in California, one at Michigan State, and another at John Jay in Manhattan. Joseph was accepted by all three, but with the desire to distance himself from home, he was left with two options: California and Michigan. With California being as distant from New York as another country, the decision boiled down to a process of elimination, leading Michigan to win by default.

There was a moment when Joseph found himself beneath the steady hum of fluorescent lights, seated at the cluttered desk of a guidance counselor, facing a choice. He sat there, weighing the idea of packing up his dreams and returning to the familiar streets of New York.

The counselor's offer had been generous, her voice soft with regret that the undergraduate program was being discontinued. She explained that introductory classes would still be offered, and going for a broader science degree could still build towards a Master's in Forensics down the line. She offered to reach out to the other schools still maintaining the program and to assist him in the transfer process if that was his choice.

A general science degree opened more doors than a niche Forensics one. Staying put and continuing on this path, even if it seemed like a temporary fix, wouldn't be such a terrible option. Joseph, at the age of eighteen, found himself at a crossroads, a decision that felt less like a choice and more like a thread unraveling. Despite being heartsick and not completely invested in the change, he took comfort in the fact that the Criminal Justice classes would still be there, even if they were only electives and not counting toward his Chemistry degree.

The reasoning behind the decision seemed solid; it wasn't like they were nudging him toward liberal arts or some other degree leading to nowhere. Chemistry still pointed toward his goal, even if the path had veered. He spent hours weighing the pros and cons, but deep down, it was all a rationalization to justify his decision to stay. The real reason cut deeper: he didn't want to go back home. Returning would feel like surrender.

There had been so much excitement flung his way when he decided to attend a "major university," as his parents called it. He could still hear the pride in their voices as they prepared him for his journey. To slink back would mean facing the sideways glances from aunts and uncles who bragged about him, or the disappointed sighs from their friends and neighbors. The expectations of what was supposed to be bigger and better things crumbling into dust.

Joseph had clawed his way out of Staten Island, a place that trapped so many in its endless cycle of strip malls and dead-end jobs. He escaped and returned like a hero, conquering distant lands. Many of his high school buddies remained ensnared in its grip, often belittling their hometown, distancing themselves, as if ashamed of their roots. They'd talk about how they were all from somewhere else, itching to leave, but they all stayed. The culture of Staten Island whispered that being from here wasn't something to flaunt: tough guys, too proud to claim it, outsiders too quick to judge it for a lack of sophistication. But through all the bluster, they never left, happy to keep prolonging their adolescence, content to go round and round in the never-ending loop of mundane city jobs and classes at C.S.I. They thought Staten Island bred the world's most exceptional assholes, but having achieved some distance, Joseph uncovered the truth. Huge assholes were not unique to Staten Island; in reality, there are assholes everywhere.

Joseph had never met a "white" person before stepping onto the campus of Michigan State University. Growing up Italian-American on Staten Island, he'd played baseball with Puerto Rican kids, celebrated bar mitzvahs with Jewish friends, and shared forties with Irish-American pals. Their skin echoed his olive tone, yet their cultures stood apart, vivid, distinct worlds etched into his mind.

Back then, "white" was a vague notion, a checkbox on a form: mark it and move on. It never aligned with the life he knew. The diversity of his community defied simple labels. How could he box people into "white" when their traditions and stories danced to such different rhythms?

On Staten Island, meeting someone new often came with a question: "What are you?" It wasn't about color; it was an invitation to claim your culture. People, whether mixed or purebred, traded heritage in percentages. You'd hear, "I'm mostly Irish, but a quarter German on my mom's side," or proud boasts like, "I'm 100% Sicilian." Even Joseph's "black" friends broke it down, Jamaican, Haitian, Dominican roots spilling out with ease.

For Joseph, it was a natural icebreaker. But at Michigan State, his first attempt with his roommate hit a wall. A wide-eyed, slack-jawed stare met his question, catching him off guard. The boy didn't know his own origins; Michiganders shared a consistent 'white' identity, and there was nothing else to it. The more Joseph asked around the dorm, the more he realized that his roommate's reaction wasn't an isolated incident. They all shrugged with the same blank frowns, clueless. He felt like an alien in a strange, honky world.

Once, he unintentionally offended a fellow student. Spotting a guy with dark skin and a Tigers cap, he pegged him as Filipino. Not wanting to assume, he extended a hand with a casual, "So, what are you?" The guy stiffened, grip tightening like a cornered stray. Confused, Joseph offered his own roots. Turns out, the Michigander had never been asked that by a "white" person. He also had never met a "white" person who identified himself as something else first. It was all very strange for both of them, but they ended up sparking a friendship. After that, Joseph held back on asking anyone about their ethnicity until he first sized up their personalities.

He hit his stride eventually. His accent and demeanor placed him apart, so he decided to own the outsider status and lean into their prejudices. Growing up the son of a performer, Joseph knew how to work a room when needed. Most interactions fizzled with a nod and a 'see ya around'. He reminded himself he wasn't there to make friends; he was there for the degree.

For his peers, freshman orientation was a first taste of freedom. Joseph watched, stunned, as they drowned in alcohol-soaked chaos, naive, sheltered kids untested by the world he knew. He'd navigated keg parties since high school, mastering moderation through trial and error. Also being raised in the shadow of Manhattan's late-night pulse, he attended some of the wildest clubs - a legendary string of hedonism and music, including places such as The Exit, The Palladium, The Tunnel, The Roxy, and Sound Factory. But his favorite den of debauchery was The Limelight. Located inside the bones of an old church, any religious person would be aghast at the modern communions taking place within. Less reckless than his friends, he still savored the whirl of dancing, drinking, and flirting.

Among the tighter bonds he forged at Michigan State, there tended to be small pockets with those who, like him, hailed from specific cultural backgrounds. He joined the brothers at Sigma Alpha Mu, a traditionally Jewish fraternity that felt reminiscent of his buddies back home. He also clicked with students from Detroit and Chicago, big city kids who got each other, once they got over the fact he wasn't black. It worked for a while, keeping his heart at arm's length from his "friends." Until Bella came around and messed it all up.

Amid the second-largest undergraduate class in the nation, he stumbled upon the one Italian girl in the whole damn place. Suddenly, he stopped obsessing over the end of his college journey and started savoring the little goals toward it. Sure, there were others with names that ended in a vowel, but being in the Midwest, the letters seemed like they'd been plucked from a game show rather than a part of their blood. They were *Eye-talians*, not Italians, jar-sauce *guineas* operating as "white." Joseph, Neapolitan on his mother's side, Barese on his father's, knew a real *paesan* when he met one. These *Eye-talians* would never understand the subtle differences within, like Sicily being considered its own thing or knowing the difference between Calabrese and Polentoni. The Midwest *Eye-talians* stayed connected to the culture by name and name alone.

Bella, despite growing up in that environment, at least comprehended what it meant to be Italian, even if she wasn't raised around it. Her parents had done an admirable job of instilling in her a notion that her lineage is not only a vestige of some ancient past, but it's something to be proud of. Over her bunk, she pinned a green, white, and red flag, and she made Joseph feel at home in the culture-starved flatlands of Michigan.

In a frame almost an inch shy of five feet, Bella is tiny but tenacious. Her raven hair surrounds a pale face. A tiny scar, left over from a dog bite when she was young, sits right above her lip. It doesn't take away, but only deepens a beauty that is uniquely hers.

To make extra cash, she worked at a phone bank, where rows of operators cold-called prospective clients for whatever company footed the bill. Her voice, smooth as worn leather, roughened at the edges by the slow burn of cigarettes, helped make her one of the top earners. Each time she was due to get off, Joseph carved a path through the snow-dusted streets of East Lansing, half a mile of frozen silence broken only by the steady crunch of his boots.

The walk was lonely, bitter, dark, and cold. The calm snowfall stuck to his scarf, the bite of icy air gnawing at his cheeks, sharp and relentless. Yet there at journey's end, her smile waited. A light strong enough to melt winter's oppressive shroud. Those long walks back through the wintry campus, deep in conversation, his girl holding snugly to his arm, linger as the warmest memories he keeps of her.

He couldn't wait for her to join him in New York. She'd fit like a glove, finally surrounded by people who'd get her. He wanted her to love the city, the people, the rough edges that shaped him.

One Christmas season, when she was in to visit, he gifted her orchestra seats to the *Phantom of the Opera*. His future shone at him as he watched the joy in her face, her eyes twinkling against the Times Square lights. Until then, Joseph entertained the idea of staying in Michigan, creating a family where she felt comfortable, and building a home with Bella there. However, now he knew better; her visit solidified his perspective. Bella would thrive in

New York, like Ole Blue Eyes said, "If you can make it here, you can make it anywhere." So, with his mind locked in and Bella by his side, the rest of his college days felt easier.

A tap on his shoulder startles Joseph. He turns to see Anthony. His reflections about Bella camouflaged his brother's approach. Glancing back at the computer screen, he realizes the Word document remains as blank as when he opened it.

"Hey, can I get on Instant Messenger? You've been on this thing all day," Anthony says, tapping his shoulder again.

Eyeing the clock, Joseph is surprised by how much time has slipped away. "Sure, sorry. Yeah, I'm just trying to... You know what, forget it." He closes down Word and launches AIM for his brother.

Anthony slides into the chair, settling in front of the dusty keys. "Ew, the seat's warm," he remarks.

Chuckling, he watches Anthony log in with the username Anaconda10, a not-so-clever reference to his man parts, no doubt. Joseph's stomach rumbles. "Hey, you want anything from the kitchen?" he asks.

"No, I'm good," Anthony says, fingers flying fast over the keys. *Probably some epic chatter for the ages*, Joseph thinks. Y2K looms, but Anthony's determined to make the most of the digital fun before the machines conk out and the world comes crashing down.

J oseph hangs up the phone, a subtle frown tugging at the corners of his mouth. He doesn't like lying to Bella. It wasn't a blatant fib to reassure her that everything's great at home, more a gentle dodge. He doesn't want her to catch on; he's second-guessing escaping Michigan. He's been stuck on the paths not taken; *what-if* scenarios haunt his thoughts.

Joseph didn't attend college on scholarship, and for now, the stacked-up debt payments are held at bay. He knows they'll hit his mailbox soon, persistent suitors clamoring for attention. He winces, seeing John Jay's cheaper tuition flash in his mind. Transferring would've lightened his financial load. The thought twists into another: maybe he should go back to Michigan, spare himself the ache of missing her. A weight in his gut heavier than any debt.

Everything happens for a reason, the mantra plays on a loop as if to convince himself. It's going to work out. He left New York to figure out how to carry his own weight and, of course, fall in love. Returning home means rejoining his family's quiet climb in America, each generation creating opportunities for the next. That's how he grew up, and how he hopes to continue when his time comes. Besides, even though he wants to be by Bella's side at every moment, he could never really blend into Michigan's fabric; he'd always be the outsider. Bella, though, is going to thrive here. He grins, picturing her beside him at the table.

Joseph compiles a list of pharmaceutical labs, many of them across the water in New Jersey. He plans to send out his resume once it's complete, but with the household's lone computer in use, it'll have to wait for another time. Unsure of how to fill the rest of the day and wanting to get out of his head, Joseph decides to do something he's never done before: treat the Island as if he's a tourist, which, ironically enough, he's beginning to feel like anyway.

Amidst the ocean's briny grip, the Island hides gritty treasures and whispered histories. Joseph drives the van down Hylan Boulevard, passing by the imposing Mount Loretto Cathedral, a monolith oddly placed among emerald slopes and towering trees. Across the boulevard, an abandoned orphanage overlooks the ocean from its hilltop perch. Long ago, it sheltered the city's destitute children, treating them so harshly that even *Oliver Twist* might've called it a getaway.

The sun crests over the salt-worn bluffs, a radiant glow casts over the water, painting the sky in hues of orange and blue. Its radiance highlights the historic Conference House. On September 11, 1776, the house bore witness to a failed treaty. Benjamin Franklin, faced his British counterparts, striving to halt the revolution. Sitting on the nearby stones, Joseph almost hears the murmurs of old debates. He contemplates the weight those learned men must have felt by the failure of their efforts. In that defeat, the exceptional nature of America was born, shaping the course of history. The house stands as a timeless tribute to the borough's enduring legacy, to persevere through defeat.

Bored and craving company, Joseph continues his aimless drive, squinting at the scenery. Lush parks wedged between cement walkways, a distinct contrast against the bustling concrete of the other boroughs. The cacophony of children's high-pitched squeals echoes as they play on swings and slides, their parents gossiping on nearby benches. Tight communities with charming streets, welcoming stoops, and a close-knit embrace.

Track-suited *goombas* bellow with laughter, scratching lotto tickets, their conversations loud enough for everyone to hear. At the mall, goth kids huddle outside Hot Topic, cigarette smoke shielding them from other shoppers. Women draped in leopard print glide with the sophistication of runway pros, their clothes hugging curves like a second skin. Frazzled mothers maneuver strollers laden with bags, their children darting ahead, prompting pleas for restraint. Young girls giggle and nod, catching the eye of young boys feigning indifference, secretly basking in the attention. And of course, the *cugini,* the tough guys, the wannabes. Teen-aged alpha males in training, muscles pumped on gym candy, tight guinea tees, and flashy gold chains. They strut in packs, hair gelled to perfection, cologne thick as a warning. Proto-men grappling with the concept of masculinity, conflating image with action. While Joseph doesn't appreciate their ostentatious style, he grins, finding more in common with the swagger of these showy assholes than the country-dwelling jerk-offs he left in Michigan.

Inspiration strikes. An old feeling he hasn't had in years. Joseph once fancied himself a poet, using his words to steer through life's mess. In recent years, nothing; the itch to put pen to paper? Gone. Now it returns like a roundhouse kick to the chest. He searches his pockets for an old receipt, a napkin, a dollar bill - anything. He finds a lone pencil, but nothing to use it on. He skips over thoughts of being home or a connection to his brothers; an image of Bella booms loudest. *But everything was fine with her,* he thinks. *So why this compulsion?* Nevertheless, the thought persists, and her name bounces around his skull:

Bella,

Bella,

Bella.

On and on and on and on.

Repetition is the key. Lock into a horse stance, keep your muscles taut. Square up the knuckles, ensuring the front two will strike true. *Punch through the target, not at it.* Repeat. Jab, cross, duck under, slide, hook. Again. Front kick, back to chamber, sidekick, back to chamber, roundhouse kick, back to chamber. Switch legs.

The basement served as the brothers' personal dojo, a space where their father drilled into them the importance of knowing how to use their hands. Boys get into fights; it's inevitable. They'd count to ten in Japanese: *Ichi, ni, san, shi, go, roku, shichi, hachi, kyu, ju;* a tradition carried over from Joseph Sr.'s own karate days.

There isn't much time in Joseph Sr.'s schedule to keep up with their training, but the muscle memory remains. Things have been tight, so he's taken dock work at St. Johnsbury for extra cash. Joseph isn't sure what his father's responsibilities are there; he only knows he gets home late - tired, dirty, and in a bad mood about it.

Lucas and Anthony, wearing gloves and headgear, are play-fighting with the equipment in a way their father wouldn't approve. The heavy bag, dragged out of hibernation, lies on the floor near the pool table.

"What's with the bag?" Joseph asks, eyeing the unused gear.

"Couldn't get it up," Lucas replies, his breath coming in short bursts. "So I decided Tony is a good enough punching dummy." He snaps a front kick at Anthony, who sidesteps it with ease.

"The bag isn't the only thing you can't get up," Anthony fires back. Lucas swipes away a punch, his irritation growing.

The fight is pure sparring; light taps, no true force behind the attacks. It's an idea born out of boredom, not any real desire to train.

"I'll help get the bag up; got next round," Joseph offers, trying to join in.

Lucas side-eyes him, his expression unreadable. "Nah, we're almost done here," he growls, his voice low and dismissive. He amps up and lands a solid sidekick square into Anthony's chest.

Anthony stumbles back, crashing into the French closet door, popping it off its track.

"Asshole," Anthony yells, grabbing for the door as it slips and clatters on the tile.

"Whatever, I'm out," Lucas snaps, throwing off his gloves and headgear. He leaves them in a messy pile on the floor and storms out.

Joseph surveys the chaos Lucas abandoned and joins Anthony in fixing the door.

SEVEN

PEPINO

Angie deals the cards to her sons, passing the time as they wait for their father to finish getting ready. She only needs another 100 points to claim her win, and when it comes to 500 rummy, she reigns as the card-table queen. Angie plays a weekly game with her friends, each taking turns to host in a round-robin fashion. On her nights, the boys know better than to bother her with trivialities; her card games are sacred lady time. She slams a winning hand down, laughing at another victory as Hot 97 spells out Method Man's name over the airwaves. The game stretches on, the clock ticking past 3 p.m.

The weighty footfalls of Joseph Sr. descend the stairs, accompanied by a gruff bark that cuts the air. "Let's go! Your grandmother wanted us there at three."

He doesn't glance back toward the kitchen; he pushes forward, out the door, and into the car. The faint hum of the Altima's engine fills the driveway.

Her husband's bossy streak is a quirk Angie giggled at in their teenage years. While his sheer force of personality works in business, guiding his bandmates with ease, it often leaves her annoyed within their household.

Angie doesn't need much time to primp, blessed with timeless charm. Even now, in middle age, her skin remains wrinkle-free, her round cheeks glowing with innocent beauty. Her husband, however, shows the years; thinning hair dyed to hide the grays, extra weight softening a frame once chiseled by GoJu-Ryu training. His wild rebel mane, once swept back with pride in his youth, is now a subject of careful grooming. He spends ages at the mirror, brush in one hand, blower in the other, ensuring each strand falls just so. In the end, despite all the effort, the results remain the same. With the rest of the household ready and killing time, he leans on the horn as if *he's* the one kept waiting.

"Alright, we're coming. Sheesh," Anthony mutters, tossing what he's sure is a winning hand down onto the table. Angie sweeps up the remaining cards, taps the deck into a neat square in the center, and follows Joseph and Anthony out of the house. Lucas stays seated in the kitchen, his eyes angling to a corner where a small spider spins its delicate web.

"Where's your brother?" Joseph Sr. directs his question at the boys through the open car door.

"Who cares?" Joseph replies, shrugging.

Joseph Sr. peers into the rearview mirror, his blue eyes boring into his sons. "Go get him."

Anthony exits the car and heads back to hurry Lucas along. Joseph meets his father's gaze in the mirror. *Lucas always stirs the pot. Dad never seems to catch on.*

"Just an observation," Joseph says, his voice careful, "but I noticed that in this family we tend to put the emphasis on the other person."

His father's eyes flicker, like he misses the point. "Like, just now, Lucas is my brother instead of your son."

"He is your brother," his mother adds, baffled.

"Yeah, I know," Joseph continues, fumbling for the right words. "But it's more than that; it's not just about the brother thing. Like, if I'm talking to my brothers, they'll say 'your mother' or 'your father' instead of just 'mom' or 'dad'." He trails off, his words stumbling, falling short of what he means.

Anthony rushes out of the house, blurting, "He's in the bathroom," cutting off his father's next command.

As the Nissan's engine hums impatiently in the driveway, the muffled sound of a flushing toilet drifts from inside.

Lucas emerges from his grandmother's bathroom and rejoins the dinner table, humming with chatter from the rest of his extended family. The dining room brims with multiple generations, a typical gathering for the weekly afternoon dinner. Though Sunday is the Lord's Day, in this family, missing mass is more forgivable than skipping Grandma's home-cooked meal. The tradition holds more significance than any devotion to the church. It's around this table they feel a sense of grace, a ritual fueling them to face the challenges of the world.

The table groans under small and large platters, steaming with red sauce-covered delights, complete with a variety of meat dishes, portions of pasta, potatoes, and salads. Most of the pan-fried meatballs, hard-crusted with delicate chewy centers, are snatched from the stove by the grubby fingers of impatient children before they can reach the adults. The day unfolds, dish after dish, thickening the air with garlic and basil, a constant service conjured by Grandma's kitchen magic. The meal culminates in the satisfying sweetness of black coffee, pastries, nuts, and fruits.

For Joseph, these gatherings always follow a similar pattern, the only notable change being the setting. Prior to college, there would be the long journey back to the Old Country and Gravesend. Since being away, the rest of the family has finally bid farewell to Brooklyn, traveling over the Narrows and settling a few blocks away on the Island.

Grandma now lives in the side apartment of her youngest, his Uncle Luke, a cozy nook where the scent of tomato sauce mingles with the static radio hum of Yankee games. This setup serves a dual purpose: helping the single father raise his four children, ages sixteen to nine, and keeping Grandma near her other grandchildren. Aunt Cici, her eldest, stops over so often she may as well have a bedroom. Her own home is quiet now, daughters flown off to their own nests, married and growing the next generation of the family.

In times past, when Grandma's parents were alive, there was a moment when all her children and grandchildren lived together under one roof. A house bursting from a chorus of voices and elbowed chaos, a tight-knit tangle they couldn't imagine unraveling. It's what one did when called to the task; she'd tie her apron and set the table. When the war broke out, her husband had to go. She dropped out of school, went to work, and set the table. When her sister died, and her parents needed to be taken care of, she moved in, cared for each of them, and set the table. When her children couldn't afford to endure on their own, she kept them together and set the table. And now, with her husband's recent passing, she shoulders the responsibility of guiding them through challenges, sickness, death, and turmoil to keep them as a united whole. Not three separate families linked by blood, but one cohesive family that shares meals, shares experiences, and stands together. She sets the table, and she's determined to keep it that way.

During his time away, Joseph missed countless birthdays, Easters, Thanksgivings, and other celebrations, too. But what he missed the most were the familiar sounds of these Sundays: the clinking of flatware, the loud, overlapping chatter, the rhythmic rise and fall of chairs as his younger cousins fidgeted like coiled springs. His gaze drifts to the vacant chair at the head of the table, a position once reserved for his grandfather. Memories flood his mind, smudging the edges of now. He sees the table as it was five years ago: cousins younger, aunts and uncles youthful, his grandfather sitting there, pride in every crinkled line of his smile. The mirage fades as his Uncle Rich, now the oldest male, takes the seat.

Aunt Cici places her hand over her nephew's and gives it a gentle shake. Joseph shifts, wondering if she caught his flinch at watching her husband take the chair or if she instinctively knows he needs a connection. She cradled him as a baby when the priest cleansed away his original sin, and she's always treated him like the son she never had. His aunt has a way of making him feel important, a special connection between godparent and godchild.

"So, Joseph, how's Bella?" she asks, a warm smile on her face.

"She's great, just great. I talked to her the other day." She squeezes Joseph's hand.

"That's good. I like that girl. She's good for you," Aunt Cici nods, squeezing again.

"Yeah, yeah, I know," Joseph exhales, relieved. Bella will fit in easily, welcomed like one of their own. His people like her, or at least appreciate the positive impact she's having on him.

"So, what have you done job-wise?" Uncle Luke's abrupt pivot jars him.

"A what?" Joseph manages, his voice almost above a whisper.

"Reggio here is a chemist," Uncle Luke points out. Joseph blinks, looking at his distant cousin for the first time in years. Reggio's grandfather, still in Italy, is a first cousin of Joseph's grandmother. Though they've crossed paths, Reggio isn't as regular a fixture in his life as his first cousins are. Born in Canada to Italian immigrants, his path to the U.S. was anything but smooth. Reggio was born with English as a second language and was smuggled in through a long drive orchestrated by Joseph's grandfather, using swapped passports bearing Joseph's information. A happy surprise to see him at the table today, but Joseph suspects a hidden agenda. As godmother, Aunt Cici tends his heart; as godfather, Uncle Luke frets over his day-to-day.

"What about you? What about where you work?" Grandma chimes in, placing a fresh serving of baked eggplant parm over Reggio's shoulder.

"Yeah, give me your resume. I'll see what I can do. I'll look around for openings," Reggio offers, digging into the dish and plopping down a healthy portion onto his plate.

"Thanks, I appreciate it," Joseph replies. Now he actually has to make a resume for real.

Aunt Cici, eager to ditch the job talk, steers back to her favorite topic, "So, what have you been doing with yourself?"

"Not much, really. Just hanging around," Joseph admits with a slight shrug.

Angela, his cousin, Anthony's age, asks, "Do you ever see any of your old friends?" At sixteen, she's already being scouted by colleges.

Joseph hesitates, softening his tone. "Not really. People tend to go their separate ways after high school, you know? You kind of lose touch." He stares at his plate, sighs, and a faint smile flickers. "I've hung out with my cousin Michael a few times, but aside from that, I'm not really going out much these days," he adds, trying to relate without sounding like a complete loser.

"Oh, Michael. What's he been doing?" Aunt Cici perks up at the name. Michael, a few years older, is Joseph's cousin on his mother's side, unrelated by blood to the Sunday dinner crew. Still, his father's side cares, as they've watched him grow since he was in diapers.

"He works for the government," Joseph says, his tone cryptic.

"Oh, what does he do?" Aunt Cici prods.

"All I can say is he transports important documents," Joseph replies, a mischievous glint in his eye.

"He's a mailman," Joseph Sr. interjects, unable to resist spilling the beans, dismantling Joseph's playful mystery.

Sofia, Angela's little sister, jumps in, "You like being back, though, right?"

Joseph forces a grin, but if even Sofia catches the drift, he's letting it slip. "Yeah, I love being home," he affirms, overcorrecting while forcing a toothy smile. "You're going to high school in the fall, right?"

Sofia nods double time, beaming. "Yeah, I'm going to Sea, like Angela."

"Oh, are you going to play ball or do any sports?" Joseph asks, curious if she'll follow her sister's path.

"Yes, cheerleading," Sofia replies, shoulders back, head high.

"Cheerleading? You're not going to do any sports?" His eyebrows raise as he scans the table. Softball is a sport; soccer is a sport. Cheerleaders are glorified spectators.

"Cheerleading is a sport!" Sofia insists, leaning in, voice rising.

"Hold up, cheerleading is not a sport," Lucas interjects, tone dripping with expertise.

"It is so! It's tough to do," Sofia counters.

"Well, just because something's tough to do doesn't make it a sport," Anthony chimes in.

"Cheerleading is a sport!" Sofia's voice climbs, breath huffing.

"Nope," Lucas retorts, putting down a fork and then crossing his arms.

"It is! It is! Arghhhh!" Sofia pulls at her hair, casts her eyes to her sister, then back at the boys.

"This denial of yours is so sad," Joseph laughs. A little teasing never hurt anybody.

The screen door screeches open, the aluminum frame clanging, and Nattie shimmies through with a bundled treasure in her carriage. At twenty-five, she's the firstborn of Joseph's generation. Her husband, John, follows, a folded playpen in one arm, a diaper bag slung over the other, dark circles under his eyes.

Baby Naomi's arrival sends a charge through the room. Her tiny fingers squeeze Grandma's, her first great-grandchild, and in those stubby digits, her fragile grip tethers the family's next chapter.

Joseph's grandfather never got to hold her properly, but in a way, she's known to him. Nattie and John learned they were expecting around the time of his passing. At his funeral, they placed the first sonogram printout into his casket. John held his cold hand, wept, and introduced his great-granddaughter to him. A promise to honor the man who'd welcomed him since he started dating Nattie at twelve.

"Oh my God, the baby! I haven't seen her yet," Joseph exclaims, eyes brightening as he rises to greet Nattie and kiss her cheek.

"Get out! I can't believe it," Aunt Cici pish-poshes, eyes misting as she watches her godson hold her grandchild.

John greets Grandma in the kitchen with a quick kiss and a playful smack on her bottom, his jovial ways bringing a smile to her face. Joseph kisses the baby's cheek, cupping her head with care, afraid any little move might hurt her. As he dances his fingers in front of her face, the screen door swings open again, grabbing his attention. Frisco slides in.

"Hey, how's everybody?" Frisco announces, greeted by waves and shouts.

"The fun never stops around here, huh?" Reggio chuckles, his accented tone adding to the spirit.

Frisco can't resist busting balls. He mimics Reggio's accent. "So, uhhhh, housed it go-in? Uhhhh, Comb-eh see key ahhh ma." His teasing sparks laughter as he b-lines to Reggio and wraps his arms around him.

Joseph shifts in his seat, watching Frisco worm into his family's affections, sliding into his chair, helping himself to food, blending into their rhythm as if he's always been there. The table is meant for guests, an extra chair always open, but it doesn't stop a pang of agita from tightening his throat. *Didn't this kid have a home of his own?* He clenches his jaw, a knot in his chest. It's annoying enough that Frisco is like a constant shadow at his mother's table, and for that, Joseph blames Lucas. But this is different. This is Sunday dinner, time for the Family, with a capital F.

Sofia, sensing allies with Nattie, John, and Frisco present, resumes her debate. "Okay, Nattie, is cheerleading a sport or not?"

"Sure, why not?" Nattie replies, rocking her daughter, absorbed by her smile.

"You see, it is," Sofia asserts, posture firming, voice victorious.

John, catching the thread, lets food spill from his mouth as he chimes in, "No, it isn't."

The boys might be against her, but with Nattie's backing, Sofia doubles down. "Well, Mrs. Hunt says it is."

"Who's that? Mike's sister?" Uncle Rich joins from across the table.

"Mike who?" Aunt Cici quizzes, knowing her husband's stupid grin means an immature punchline is coming.

Uncle Rich cocks his head, slowing his pace. "Mrs. Hunt. Her brother, Mike." Aunt Cici braces. "Angie knows him."

Angie, about to eat, lowers her fork. "Who do I know?"

Joseph catches the setup, scanning for knowing expressions.

"Mrs. Hunt's brother, Mike," Uncle Rich clarifies, baiting her.

"Ma, don't," Joseph warns, but it's too late.

"Mike Hunt, I don't know a Mike Hunt," Angie says, falling into the trap. Her eyes widen as she realizes, face flushing tomato-red. "Oh, you ass," she mock-scolds Uncle Rich, who laughs.

At the other end, away from the napkin beating Uncle Rich gets from Angie and Aunt Cici, Joseph sits near Lucas and turns to Frisco.

"So, what were you guys up to last night?" Joseph asks.

Lucas, the master of vagueness, offers, "We went out."

"With whom?" Joseph presses.

"People," Lucas deadpans.

"Ah, of course," Joseph claps. "Let me guess, you did stuff with things," he says, waving his hands like a street magician hawking his next trick. Lucas giggles despite himself.

The laughter spreads to Frisco, eyes darting between the brothers. Lucas covers his mouth, and Joseph grows more animated. "You guys are too much," Frisco adds.

"Oh, you don't even know the half of it," Joseph continues. "We passed a restaurant the other day."

"This is funny," Lucas chuckles, shaking a finger at his friend.

"Lucas says he knows someone who works there." Joseph lifts his shoulders, looking from Frisco to Lucas and back.

"So I ask. Who?" Joseph turns his hand over, offering the floor.

"People," Lucas deadpans.

Joseph drives it home. "Of course, it's good to know people. Because if you knew the chairs and food and shit, I don't see how that would help you."

He slaps the table, and the three share a laugh. *Maybe this Frisco kid is alright after all.*

"You have to admit, you guys might fight, but when you're together, you're hysterical," Frisco remarks, wiping a tear.

But then again, maybe not. "I'm glad we can make your day," Joseph finishes, laughter dying like a flipped switch. His squabbles with Lucas aren't a show for this kid's amusement.

Vincent, a restless spark and the youngest cousin at nine, tugs at Joseph's shirt. "Joe, you wanna go outside and play baseball?"

Joseph takes in Vincent's doe-eyed, chubby-faced grin and, guilted by his pleading eyes, nods. "Sure, who's playing?"

Dented yellow plastic bats, slitted white plastic balls, gray parked cars, and a rusted free-standing basketball hoop slot in for the traditional base paths and equipment of a proper game. The uneven diamond stretches out, with first base, a Johnny Pump, farther from second base, a large rock on the ground, then second is from third, the basketball hoop.

Joseph and Lucas captain the teams, splitting the players evenly. Lucas wins the first pick by chance and chooses Frisco. Joseph counters with his brother Anthony. Lucas snatches Angela, rounding out the core of his squad. The remaining spots on each four-person team go to the younger cousins. Since Lucas has the stronger players, he's given the weakest, Vincent, to balance things out, leaving Joseph with Sofia and her twelve-year-old brother, Little Joseph.

Little Joseph, formerly known as Baby Joseph, stands in the batter's box, clutching the yellow bat. He smacks it against home plate, a cut-up piece of cardboard. Not long ago, the family had four Josephs. Back then, their grandfather was Big Joseph, Joseph was Little Joseph, and the youngest was Baby Joseph. Now, with their grandfather gone, the names have shifted: Joseph Sr. is Big Joseph, Little Joseph is adjectiveless Joseph, and Baby Joseph has graduated to Little Joseph.

"I wanna pitch! Lucas, let me pitch. I'm pitching next!" Vincent tugs at Lucas's arm, breaking his focus mid-windup.

"Vincent, if you don't be quiet, I'm going to hang you by your underwear from the basketball hoop," Lucas warns.

Little Joseph doubles over, laughing at the image of Vincent dangling.

Vincent, taxing the limit of his nine-year-old wit, shoots back. "Quiet! At least I *have* underwear."

"What? What does that mean? That doesn't make any sense," Little Joseph says, shaking the bat at him.

"Oh yeah? Oh yeah? You don't have underwear because you don't have a penis," Vincent declares, fist pumping like he's won. After all, everyone knows boys are supposed to have penises.

"Yeah, I do. His name is Vincent," Little Joseph grins.

Vincent's hands drop, his face flushing as laughter erupts around him. He shakes his head, scrambling for a comeback.

Vincent, desperate not to appear weak, charges his brother. Head down, arms pumping, legs churning like pistons, he barrels forward. Angela scoops him up mid-stride, spinning him around. She puts him down and kneels to his level.

"Cut it out! Are we playing or not?" she says, her tone firm but kind.

As the oldest of Uncle Luke's four, Angela leads the pack. From a young age, she's been both big sister and substitute mother, loving them fiercely but tolerating none of their nonsense, especially when there's a game to be played.

Lucas readies himself and pitches, making quick work of Little Joseph with three consecutive strikes. He throws the bat down and slumps on the curb, frowning.

"Alright, Sofia, you're up next!" Joseph calls, handing her the bat.

Sofia steps in, and Lucas squints. He shifts his stance, circling the wiffle ball in his palm. "Okay, Sofia, you're up. What position are you playing? Let's see, is it first or second cheer?" he quips.

Sofia sticks her tongue out, prances out of the box, takes a practice swing, and sways back in.

Lucas delivers the ball. Sofia connects hard, sending it into play. Frisco flicks his hand up, the slap of the plastic to flesh audible as he snags the line drive. Sofia, only two steps into her run, huffs and joins her brother on the curb.

With two outs and no one on, Vincent runs in from the field. "Now I pitch!" he demands, reaching for Lucas.

Lucas spins and hurls the ball at Vincent, pelting his shoulder. The ball bounces off, birthing a round red mark on the soft tissue in its wake. Vincent stomps, a tear rolling down as he bolts inside.

"Why'd you do that for?" Anthony asks from the batter's box.

Lucas throws again, this time at Anthony's head. Anthony ducks, and the ball skips down the street. Little Joseph and Sofia race after it.

"You're such a jerk," Anthony says, ears turning pink.

Joseph places a hand on Anthony's shoulder and shrugs. "Vincent was being annoying."

Sofia reaches the ball and laughs in victory.

"You don't understand. He's always a jerk," Anthony mutters, jaw tight.

Little Joseph sits back on the curb as Sofia sashays over, hands on her hips, staring him down.

Lucas catches the ball from Sofia and points at Anthony. "Why don't you cry about it? Oh, wait, let me run inside so you can call Jackie," he taunts.

Anthony stands in the batter's box as the sun dips, shadows stretching across the asphalt. A tumbleweed rolling past wouldn't feel out of place as the brothers lock eyes. "Just pitch the ball," Anthony says.

Lucas hurls the ball through the charged air. Anthony swings the bat as an extension of his body. The yellow bat cracks against the ball with a sharp *thwack*. It rockets past the players, bouncing and rolling far down the street. Angela chases after it. Anthony rounds the bases, fist raised, as Lucas yells at Angela to hurry. Anthony touches home plate, triumphant.

Every problem plaguing New York and the grand fixes for the whole world unfold over plates of baked breaded chicken simmering in onions and roast beef steeped in a thick gravy of flour and its own juices.

Uncle Luke, whose teenage years were shaped in Brooklyn's simmering streets of the 1970s, can't shake the weight of old grudges. Uncle Rich, an electrician and a union man to his core, always votes blue, sparking clashes with Joseph Sr.'s harder-edged conservative streak. The conversation volleys fast, critiques of pop culture and politics lobbed like a table tennis rally: Uncle Luke's serve, Joseph Sr.'s return. Yet, it always loops back to one bitter note.

"How are you going to live like that, act like animals to your own people, and still make anything of yourself?" Uncle Luke spits, his scorn for the projects and their residents dripping from every word.

"It's not even the blacks, it's everything," Joseph Sr. says, jabbing his fork at his younger brother. "Nobody cares anymore, not even the Italians."

Uncle Luke nods, brow creasing deep. "They let all these foreigners in here. And for what?"

Joseph Sr. leans back, blue eyes cutting past his brother's anger. "Our grandfather was a foreigner."

"Not like today's," Uncle Luke waves him off, slamming his hand on the table. "He came here to be here, to be a part of this country."

Grandma, hands still damp from the sink, sits next to Joseph Sr. and wipes them on a napkin. "My father came and made it without any of this welfare because he worked hard his whole life to speak English and be American."

Uncle Rich shakes his head, jaw tight. "It's a disgrace what's happened to the mentality in this country. Nobody cares."

Joseph Sr. locks eyes with his brother-in-law. "What do you expect when Democrats hand everything out? I just don't like that they think it's their right to get what I worked for. And you're right, the blacks may have it the worst. I feel bad for the ones that try to make something of themselves when so many of them act like degenerates."

Grandma gets her worldview from TV, tabloids, and Uncle Luke's complaints, finding his opinions as juicy as celebrity gossip or the troublemakers on the 6 o'clock news. "And that Sharpton, what a loudmouth."

Joseph Sr. pats her hand, drying a spot she missed. "I'll tell you something, ma. They don't even like him."

Uncle Luke scoffs. "No, he's an instigator. He complains. He marches. And where does it get anybody? Nowhere."

Grandma's heard it all before. She rolls her eyes at the excuses. There's no time for people pointing fingers, blaming others for their troubles. She's lived through poverty, lost family too soon, watched her father struggle, and now sees her son go through it. No matter how dirt-stained their clothes, no matter how drawn their faces, they found the strength to smile for their children.

"When the Italians came to this country, they were treated like dogs. But instead of making a big stink, we worked and worked, and what happened?" She wrings the napkin in her hand, glances at her boys, then at the photographs on the wall. Her husband, forever handsome in uniform, smiles back, an American flag in a triangle mount nearby. "Look at us today. If our people could do it, any of them can."

"They're too lazy, like everybody else. The world is changing; look at things today," Uncle Luke stammers. "Technology is becoming our downfall."

"What are you talking about?" Uncle Rich, who'd been ignoring the speechifying until now, perks up. The same old complaints like a scratched record, but the technology gripe is new.

"Lucas hit me with the ball!" Vincent cries, charging through the screen door like a bull, exaggerated tears streaming.

Grandma, well-acquainted with her grandchildren's antics, reaches for a pastry and hands it to the attention-seeking child. The sweet treat works like a charm, instantly quelling his distress. He swallows the sticky delight nearly whole, and his tears stop as if a valve twisted shut.

"Technology is going to ruin the world," Uncle Luke pronounces, hands in motion as if molding his argument from thin air. "Think about it. Take your sons, for example. They didn't grow up like us."

Joseph Sr. leans in. "We didn't grow up like our parents either."

"Exactly! The next generation will never be as physically fit or have the social connection that people in the past had. You get people with this internet where they don't have to leave their house."

Joseph Sr. chuckles, catching Uncle Rich giving Uncle Luke the crazy eyes.

"Times have changed. It's not the computers. There's no sense of neighborhood anymore; people don't care about each other's kids," Uncle Rich adds. "At least back in the '60s, kids got involved. Now everyone wants to handle their own business and not be bothered."

"And it's only going to get worse. You've got these people who never leave the house, do their shopping, have their entertainment, growing soft, and nobody's left for hard labor," Uncle Luke picks up a walnut and cracks it open with a squeeze. "So, who are you going to have doing jobs that people depend on to live, like your garbage men and police? You'll have unfit, social misfits handling the things that really hold the world together." He tosses the nut into his mouth.

Joseph Sr. sips his coffee, the mug warm against his palm. "It's a different time, is all. The world is changing at an incredibly fast pace."

"Not changing, *dying*."

Vincent, licking his fingers clean, tugs at Grandma's sleeve. "Grandma, can I have another one?"

She smiles at his sugar-dusted face, eyes softening as she ruffles his hair. "Of course, sweetheart. Let me get you another." She leads him into the kitchen.

The dining room table sits barren, and the apartment has fallen into a still, post-dinner hush. There is no shuffling of feet or clinking of metal utensils on porcelain plates. No trays of food await on the countertops, no pots simmer on the stove, and no dishes stack in the sink. If a home could take a day off, this is what it would feel like.

Grandma sits at her small wooden table in the corner of the kitchen, a nook barely wide enough for three chairs but spacious enough for poring over her gossip rags. She flips through the full-color pages, lost in the glossy scandals of her soap stars. It's a delightful distraction to imagine the real-life drama unfolding behind her stories. She starts to get into a juicy bit about a secret affair when the doorbell chimes, breaking her focus.

"Hold on, hold on," she calls out, setting aside her reading glasses and magazine. She rises from her chair and makes her way to the door.

Upon opening it, she finds her grandson Joseph standing there, his gaze locked on a far-off speck in the sky. Most of her visitors drop by unannounced, a quick hello between errands. She smirks, knowing they're sneaking a peek at how she's holding up since he's been gone. She'd raised them; they should know better. She can take care of herself. Still, she's always glad to see them, though she wishes they wouldn't fret so much.

"Oh, Joseph. What are you doing here?" Grandma greets him, ushering him into a familiar embrace.

"I had nothing to do, so I thought I'd come over," Joseph replies, planting a gentle kiss on his grandmother's cheek.

She gestures toward the small table. Joseph hesitates, fingers fidgeting with the hem of his jacket. He crosses the threshold and sinks into a chair, the wood creaking faintly under his weight. The apartment lies still, save for a soft ticking from a clock on the wall, a steady pulse in the silence. He glances at the table, then out the window, avoiding her gaze.

Grandma shuffles to the kitchen counter, her slippers squeaking against the linoleum. She cracks open a cabinet and arranges small cookies onto a plate, then places it in the middle of the table and puts on a fresh pot of coffee.

"Where is everyone?" she asks, clicking on the stovetop to heat the press.

"I don't know. I woke up, and they were gone. I think my mom's shopping or something, but I don't know where my brothers went," he answers, eyes distant as he nibbles on a cookie.

Grandma leans back from the counter, her sharp eyes scanning his face. Her expression stills, though her eyes flicker with concern. His achievements have brought joy to both her and her late husband, and she is so very proud of him. He's always been an intelligent and well-behaved boy, often preferring the solace of his books over the rowdy games of the other kids. In his childhood, he'd entertain her with wild, imaginative stories. And being her blood, he was handsome to boot. She spots a shadow in his eyes, a slump in his shoulders.

She places a Las Vegas mug before him, the steam rising to tickle his nose, snapping him out of his daze. She sits down across from him with her cup and watches him sip.

Joseph mumbles, his voice quiet and unsure. He shifts, his eyes darting to Grandma's magazine stack. "Reading anything good?"

She chuckles, a dry, knowing sound, and glances over her shoulder. "Oh, just the usual nonsense. Affairs, breakups, secret babies. Keeps me out of trouble." She pauses, watching him.

Joseph's done it, she thinks. She'd been a little girl once, accepted into college. Not so long ago, really. But the war came, responsibilities piled up, and the family never made it back. Skips a generation, she guesses. Yet here he is, an accomplished man. She nods, her eyes softening; life's more than achievements. It's a tangled mess, not easily reduced to checkboxes leading to happiness. He has everything laid out for a bright future, and still, he comes to her for that missing piece. Grandma's always up to the task. After all, cookies and coffee never fail.

She cradles her mug, letting the warmth seep into her hands. She knows exactly where to start. "How's Bella?"

"She's good." Grandma notices the genuine smile curling his lips, but it downturns quickly as he adds, "Everything's good."

Joseph stares into the black of the coffee, the surface rippling in circular waves as he breathes.

"What's wrong?" she presses.

"I don't know. It's just...," For a moment, there's only the clock ticking, each second stretching the silence taut. Then he speaks, his words slow. "Things are different. She's been acting weird." Admitting it out loud makes the idea more concrete, more tangible. Now he's birthed it into the world,; he can never again pretend everything's the same. What he doesn't admit out loud is that it's not only her behavior that's changed.

"Well, Joe, I have to tell you, I like her. She's a good girl. But you had to expect something," Grandma offers.

"I know, I know. She was all I had for two years. We spent all our time together," Joseph nods.

"And now she's there all alone," Grandma smiles, her eyes folding into laughter lines, full of quiet wisdom. She recognizes a softness in his voice when he mentions her. But she also knows love's road is full of potholes, especially with distance in play. She knows better than most. Her husband far away, fighting on a foreign shore. But when he returned, their love came back with him. It's possible for Joseph, too. There's always the chance things will work out. There's a lid for every pot, as her mother used to say.

Joseph takes a sip of his coffee, its heat steadying him, and for the first time since he arrived, his gaze settles on her. Grandma reaches across the table, her hand resting lightly on his. Her skin is cool, papery, but her grip is steady. "She probably just misses you."

Joseph's eyes search hers. He hopes it's a simple matter of loneliness and longing, but he isn't convinced.

The clock ticks on. Then the screen door slams, boisterous and loud.

"Ooooohhhh, Joseph, I didn't know you were here," Angela bursts in, surprising her cousin with the strength of her embrace. She's becoming quite the softball sensation, and the bear hug crushing his ribs convinces Joseph the stories are true.

Angela reaches over, knocking Joseph aside to grab a cookie.

"Yeah, I had nothing to do today, so I thought I'd get out," Joseph replies, hiding the discomfort in his side as he sits back down.

"That's good. When you see your brother, tell him to call me," Angela directs, her words muffled by a mouthful of cookie.

"Which one?" Joseph asks, wincing.

"Who do you think? Tony!" Angela punctuates with a jab to Joseph's arm. Either he needs to go back to the gym, or Angela needs to stop; she's growing up strong.

"You guys hanging out tonight?"

Angela's eyes light up. "Yeah, me, my boyfriend Ezra, Tony, and *Jackie*."

Joseph snorts, hot coffee burning his nose as it spills onto his shirt. "Ezra!"

He grabs a napkin, wiping at the brown stain. "There are way too many people with the same name running around in my life."

The lack of original names is getting out of hand, Joseph thinks. He's already dealing with four different Josephs, two Lucases, and now the Ezras are multiplying.

Grandma takes the dirty napkins from Joseph and tosses them in the trash. "Joseph, how is Ezra?"

"He's good. His baby got so big."

Grandma's eyes sparkle, her smile widening at the news, but she can't help noticing her grandson isn't smiling.

"You got me fired up, fired up
You got me so
You got me fired up, fired up
You got me so"
-Funky Green Dogs

EIGHT

FIRED UP!

Tiny red devil horns and a mascara-curled mustache bounce down an alleyway in Gravesend. Anthony waddles, waving his candy-filled pillowcase at the video camera. A miniature Groucho Marx jumps in front of him, waving his plastic cigar as he shakes and swishes his pelvis to and fro.

"Joseph, I can't see your brother," the melodic sing-song of a young woman's voice calls from behind the camera. High-pitched giggles of children fill the cracked concrete stretch of West Street. Back then, the outside world was only as large as their Brooklyn block. Anthony's mom could only afford to make silly homemade costumes, while the other kids strolled in their plastic masks and store-bought replicas. She had him smiling and dancing, comfortable in his hand-stitched getup.

Anthony pauses, an old Halloween video flickering in his mind, a scene he rarely revisits. He was so young that his awareness of it was formed solely from home movie viewings. Something about how he's styling his hair in the bathroom dredges it up from the back of his mind.

As Whitney Houston and Deborah Cox musically debate about what role they are to play, Anthony manipulates the sticky pink gel, fingers running through the thick black darkness of his mane, taming each strand to perfection. He's putting on a costume of a different kind, this one not for his own kicks, but shaped for others' eyes.

"Tony, pick up the phone!" Lucas shouts from downstairs.

Anthony, bopping to the beat of the two divas' musical combat, only hears a muffled voice drifting upward. He sets down the hairdryer and turns the knob on the radio, lowering the volume.

Anthony leans toward the door, and "PHONE!" hits his eardrums with such clarity and force that Lucas could've been standing next to him.

Anthony slicks more gel from his temples to the back of his head. "Who is it?" he calls out, only to be rewarded with silence. "Lou?"

Anthony listens again. Nothing. "Lou!"

Lucas's feet pound up the staircase, curt and quick.

Lucas, blank as a wall, stares at his brother through the iron guardrail. "It's Jackie." He rolls his eyes, the *no-duh, who else would it be* look plain on his face.

Anthony smirks; he has other friends.

Sure, they call.

Sometimes.

Maybe.

"Tell her to come over," Anthony instructs.

Lucas hops up the last few steps, a certain spring in his movements. "I already hung up."

Lucas makes his way into the bathroom and nudges Anthony aside with his shoulder. He picks up Tony's gel and massages it into his own hair. "What are you doing tonight? Another wild night of sitting on the couch next to her?"

Anthony hip-checks Lucas, jockeying for position in front of the mirror, an arm shoving, a leg falling off balance. "Oh, so funny. I make a very special wonton soup for you." Anthony jokes, trying on his best Jerry Lewis Chinese accent.

"Actually, we're going out with Angela and Ezra, ass."

Lucas mock claps at the news, putting on an overdrawn look of excitement.

"I'm back!" Joseph announces his arrival, throwing open the creaky living room door and bounding up the stairs.

"Nobody cares," Lucas is quick to remind him.

Joseph perches on the steps, hands gripping the cold bars of the iron guardrail. He watches his two brothers like a prisoner, admiring the freedom of those on the other side. Anthony leans close to the mirror, hands tugging at his hair; Lucas sprays a sharp mist of Le Mâle cologne, dousing his neck and chest. It's like watching a ballet on the mating rituals of teenage boys.

"Did anybody call?" Joseph asks.

"Sure, lots of people," Lucas responds, eyes fixed on his primping.

"Anyone for me, ass?" The name he's been using more often for Lucas, to the point that an extra 's' might be a solid permanent addition.

"Michael called."

"What about Bella?" Joseph sighs. Getting info from Lucas is like pulling teeth. Even when he lets some tidbits escape his vault-like mind, Joseph's never sure if it's the full story.

Lucas turns his head, locking eyes with Joseph, and replies with a simple, no-snark "No."

Lucas holds Joseph's gaze for a moment, watching the irritation twitch in his jaw. Satisfied, Lucas turns back to the mirror, continuing his preparations.

Joseph abandons his journey upward and heads back down toward the kitchen.

Lucas examines the empty spot where his brother just stood. His eyes focus on the metal bars, and he shakes his head. Turning back to the mirror, he captures a fleeting glimpse of the same trapped look he'd just seen in his brother's eyes. He blinks, and it's gone. The cocky glint of the Ass Man is back, and tonight they're going to shine.

Michael's number is well-practiced, and Joseph's fingers fly over the buttons. The keys boop and bop like the first bars of a new-age song, and the phone rings twice before a familiar female voice answers: Michael's mom, his Aunt Donna.

"Hi, is Michael there?" Joseph gets right to the point, a strategy he's learned from past experiences with his aunt. It's best to navigate her conversations with directness, avoiding her habit of drifting into a conversational maze that can turn a quick hello into a half-hour of half-thoughts.

"Michael, your son," Joseph asserts, his tone firm. "It's Joseph, your nephew." He knows better than to let her drift into one of her long, winding stories. She's always been something of a dreamer, to put it nicely.

Joseph paces back and forth in the five feet of space the phone cord allows and waits. Lucas jets down from upstairs, grabs the keys to the Altima, and rushes out of the house.

"Michael! What's up?" The sound of a car horn interrupts, turning Joseph's head away from the phone.

He mouths *damn* after looking at the door and the empty hook where the Altima's keys should be.

"No, nothing, like usual. What are you up to?" The car horn blares again, lingering longer this time. "Yeah, sounds cool. Did I ever meet this kid?" Joseph continues over the noise.

Anthony races down; no more beeps, the car's blaring morphed into one long honk now. Anthony shoots out the door in a blur. The car falls silent, except for the screech of its tires as it peels out and drives off.

"Alright, yeah, come pick me up. I don't know, like an hour or so. Alright, see ya later," Joseph concludes.

With plans for the night made, Joseph hangs up the phone. He grins, realizing both of his brothers have left; he won't have to fight them for time in the mirror.

Jackie has less than a couple of seconds to leap out of the Nissan's backseat before it races off, tearing down Mason Boulevard. Anthony takes her hand, and they walk along the concrete path. Jackie reaches for the bell, but Anthony stops her, pushing the unlocked front door open with ease. Uncle Luke never locks his door; he doesn't need to. His three-story house, complete with a side apartment, sits at the end of a quiet street, flanked by a public golf course on one side, a matching detached house on the other, and greenbelt-protected woodlands stretching out behind it.

Angela bounds down the long run of steps by the foyer, tossing her cousin a quick head nod. Her eyes narrow into thin slits when she spots Jackie beside him, but out of respect for Anthony, she offers a curt wave.

Angela's smile fades as she glances at Jackie, her fingers tightening on the banister. They aren't outright enemies, but Jackie and Angela see each other as rivals. Both fierce athletes from competing high schools, Jackie can still feel the grit of dirt on her knees from their last showdown on the softball field.

Anthony's mind drifts to a tied game early in his relationship with Jackie when she and Angela collided on the diamond. Angela stood on second base, poised for the hit that could carry her to home and victory. The bat cracked sharply, the sound rising across the field as the ball sailed high and far. Angela took off second without hesitation; *no point in waiting with two out.* If the ball were caught, staying put wouldn't save her.

She either missed the third base coach trying to hold her up or flat-out ignored her. Even now, her lips press tight when anyone asks about it. She just ran, sprinting past the base, tearing down the chalked line toward home. Jackie braced herself, tracking the left fielder as she scooped up the ball and fired it her way. Angela saw it whip past her, landing in Jackie's mitt. She had two options: double back to third and risk a rundown, or charge ahead. Like a freight train, imaginary whistle screaming, Angela dropped her shoulders and plowed straight into Jackie.

The collision lifted Jackie off her feet, cleats scraping air, catcher's mask flying off her head. Anthony, watching from the stands, shielded his eyes, peeking through splayed fingers at the horror. Sprawled in the dirt, Jackie thrust her gloved hand skyward, the softball gripped tight in its webbed embrace. Angela was out, both at home plate and for the remainder of the game. The umpire sent her packing, and Jackie's team claimed the win.

The memory fades as Angela's voice slices through. "So, what did you want to do?" she asks.

"I don't know; what does Ezra want to do?" Anthony replies. The night hums with potential as they shuffle inside, Angela leading with a sly grin.

"I don't know; he's not here yet," she says.

"Okay, we'll watch TV till he gets here," Anthony decides. Angela leaps onto the couch in the TV room and flips on the set. Blue light spills from the massive screen, casting long shadows across the walls as they settle in to wait.

Michael's running late. Escaping the flood of questions his mother unleashes whenever he tries to leave the house is always a struggle. Despite the barrage, he slips away and arrives at Joseph's door.

Ringing the doorbell, Michael shuffles his feet on the scratchy, worn doormat, bracing for Joseph's signature eye-roll scowl or exasperated sigh. He stands there, thumbs twisting, his thoughts spinning like black vinyl about his cousin's reaction to his tardiness. Michael's biggest enemy is Michael. He often sees himself as a background character in others' lives; even in his own story, he doesn't claim top billing. He recalls their last hangout, cracking jokes as the wingman, stepping aside as comic relief, always the damsel awaiting rescue, waiting for the plot to unfold around him rather than because of him.

Maybe Joseph ditched me, Michael thinks. *Or he went out without me.* A ping of panic nudges his digit into pressing the doorbell again.

On the third ring, Joseph answers. Instead of the well-dressed, disappointed cousin Michael expects, he's greeted by a wet, unshaven mess, barely covered by a towel.

"You're not ready!" Michael exclaims.

"I didn't expect you to get here so quick," Joseph replies with a yawn, eyeing his cousin up and down. "You're wearing that?"

Michael glances at himself, relieved he's at least better dressed than a guy in a towel. Maybe. "What?" he retorts.

"Nothing, I..." Joseph raises an eyebrow, his gaze dropping to Michael's feet. "Sneakers, huh?"

"What's wrong with sneakers?" Michael counters, a touch defensive.

"Particularly? Nothing. Just on an occasion like going out to hang out, they're fine. However, without any set goals or plans, I can see how they might cause a problem," Joseph explains.

Michael's confusion deepens, brows knitting together. Joseph sighs. "Forget it. I'm wearing shoes..."

"Jeans too, huh?" Joseph, unrelenting, continues his appraisal.

"And what's wrong with jeans?" Michael fires back.

Joseph raises an eyebrow again. "Particularly?"

The backyard is immense but lacks grass; its gray pavement encircles a massive in-ground pool complete with a diving board. The pool sits vacant, save for a few inflatable rafts drifting by. Partygoers pose in well-dressed stances, puffing out their chests, more engrossed in their red cups than in swimming. Thumping bass and strobe-like floodlights turn the pool party into a nightclub. An oversized speaker on a duct tape-marred black pole in the corner blares Kim Sozzi's *Alone*. Gold chains and hoop earrings glint under the backyard lights, infusing the scene with touches of sparkle. Muscled torsos are accentuated by snug-fitting Armani Exchange T-shirts, unbuttoned shirts billowing around them. Hair styled with care, spikes up to the heavens, stiff enough to defy even the slightest head tilt. Ladies sport lacy tank tops cropped high above the belly button, displaying a multitude of piercings. High-cut jean shorts hug their figures, cinched with large rhinestone-studded belts of various colors. As they sway their hips to the rhythm, their shoulder-length hair brushes against black neck chokers.

Not a single bathing suit in sight.

Lucas lifts his red cup to his lips and surveys the trio of girls in front of him.

"Okay, my turn, new rule," Lucas declares, jabbing skyward with a grin. "You," he points at a stunning five-two brunette with yellow highlights and a sapphire tongue ring. "Yes, you. If every time someone says my name..." He pauses, tapping his finger against his chin. "Hmmm, what's my name?"

"Louie," a nearby blonde with a copper tan jumps in.

Lucas gestures towards the tan hottie. "Right." He redirects his attention to his brunette beauty, a dimpled smile forming. "Every time somebody says Louie," he continues, a playful glint in his eye, "you have to kiss me right on the face."

The two girls beside the brunette laugh in approval.

"That's not fair," the brunette protests.

"Them's the rules, sorry," Hatcher interjects. A proper wingman, ready to keep the game rolling.

Lucas throws his hands up in a shrug.

"Hey, Lou, pass me a beer."

At Hatcher's request, the brunette's eyes light up. "He said Louie; he should have to kiss you."

"No, he said Lou, not..." The tan blonde stops herself before saying the magic word and places a hand on her friend's shoulder. "Buuuutttt, you just said it," she points out with a giggle.

Lucas beams, points to his nose, and with his other hand, gestures toward the brunette, his smile widening.

The tan blonde shoves her friend toward Lucas, who slides in close, their bodies brushing.

Looking up at his handsome face, she can't help but crack a smile. "I did say it, didn't I?" She plants a kiss firmly on his cheek, fulfilling the rules, and then, to Lucas's delight, she continues, moving her lips to meet his.

The door creaks as Ezra opens it. He walks into the foyer and heads toward the sound of the television. Ezra, just a month past sixteen, strides in, lean and athletic. His boy-next-door face could put any playground mom at ease around her kids. His big brown eyes reflect the flickering television screen as he observes Angela, Anthony, and Jackie sprawled across the sagging, plaid couch. A goofy smile, all teeth and charm, splits his face, pairing well with the alto tones of his voice as he announces his entrance.

"Oh hey, is this still on?" Ezra exclaims, slapping Anthony five and sitting down next to Angela. "I was watching a little of this when I left my house."

Anthony watches Ezra place a chaste kiss on Angela's cheek and shifts somewhat. The wild spark he feels around Jackie seems absent in their exchange. Anthony frowns, puzzled. Ezra's a good guy, even if he is a little soft, yet Angela's always so cold to him. They look more like good friends than a couple, Anthony thinks, watching Angela remove Ezra's arm from around her shoulder.

"So, where do you want to go?" Angela asks, punching Ezra in the shoulder.

Ezra shrugs, letting Angela's punch land without a flinch; he's used to her calling the shots. "I don't care," he responds. He glances around at Anthony and Jackie. "Anybody hungry?"

"We can grab some food and figure something out along the way," Anthony chimes in, coming to Ezra's aid. He sinks deeper into the couch, arm draped around Jackie, eyes flicking to the TV; he's not ready to budge. "This movie is almost over, and then we'll head out."

Joseph and Michael cruise the moonlit streets of Staten Island in Michael's car. It's not the van, but it's not fresh off the assembly line either. The four-door sedan bears a dent on one side, the metal crumpled from some long-ago fender-bender. Copper-colored rust creeps along the edges, vivid against the dull gray paint. The car moves through the night with a stuttering blink, its sole working headlight casting a feeble glow on the darkened streets. Inside, the interior could use vacuuming. Stains of various discolorations, coffee, candy, or worse, dot the seats, sticky under Joseph's fingers. The air is stale, a mix of old Burger King and forgotten gym clothes. A faded NY METS air freshener, long past its prime, hangs from the mirror, bouncing with every dip in the pavement.

Joseph flips down the passenger-side visor mirror, splitting his fingers to smooth his eyebrows. He inspects his jaw for stray stubble he might've missed due to Michael's earlier-than-expected arrival. He couldn't locate his preferred pants, so he settled on dark jeans. He pairs them with comfortable black shoes from Aldo and a silky black short-sleeved button-down shirt from Express. Fortunately, his hair cooperates for once, a relief, since he'd noticed it thinning, blaming the stress of finals for their retreat, aghast at the horror of watching strands falling to the sink with increasing frequency. He rests a hand on his hairline, staring, tracing it with a frown.

"So, who is this girl we're meeting?" Joseph asks, closing the sun visor and turning to his cousin.

"Just a friend of mine," Michael replies, shrugging one shoulder.

"Just a friend, huh?" Joseph raises an eyebrow. He isn't buying Michael's nonchalance. It isn't like him to meet up with girls. Often when they go out, they hang with his old high school friends or post office buddies. "Nothing going on between you two?"

Michael waves away the insinuation with a chuckle. "The last time I had something going on between me and a girl was right before my mother gave me birth," he quips. His mouth twists into a half-smile, half-frown as he speaks.

"That's not true. I know you've had girlfriends," Joseph laughs.

"Yeah, like two years ago," Michael shrinks into himself, shoulders sagging.

The South Shore row of houses, with their vinyl siding and sloped roofs, morphs into sharper brick edges and compressed buildings. Joseph detects a hint of gloom in Michael's voice. He fiddles with the radio, hunting for something uptempo to lift the mood.

"Well, at least you have friends and go out. Every time we go out, we're meeting this one or that one." He leaves it on a rock station, and Nirvana's grunge riff fills the car. "This girl tonight, she cute?" Joseph asks, taking Michael's head bob as a yes. "Well, why didn't you ask her to hang out alone?"

"Ah, she wouldn't go for me," Michael says, a faint, lopsided smile tugging at his lips as he hesitates. "You know how sometimes you have dreams, and there's a beautiful woman, and they give you sex," he muses.

"A sex dream?"

"Yeah," Michael nods with a grin. "Well, I don't. When I shut my eyes, I don't see beautiful women…"

Joseph's eyes widen in mock horror. "If you tell me you see guys, I know this kid Jared you should talk to," he teases.

"No, not guys. I'm just talking about ordinary to ugly chicks; okay, mostly ugly chicks fooling around with me," Michael confesses, glancing from the road to his cousin.

Joseph's grin widens into a silent laugh, shoulders shaking. "Oh well, that ain't so bad. Ugly chicks in your dreams giving you sex," he cracks.

"You see, that's just it," Michael's face clouds over as he continues driving. "Even they reject me. I can't even make it with *fugly* chicks in my own dreams," he admits. "The closest I came was this one time I was having a dream about this girl I knew. She came over to my house and was like, 'Do me now!'"

"So, what happened?" Joseph leans in.

Michael flicks his gaze from the road to his cousin and back. He keeps his right hand on the steering wheel while painting a vivid picture with his left. "Well, I take her into my basement, and then BAM! PG-13 movie! The lights go out in my head, and all I can hear is the sounds of her moaning. That's it, no nudity, no interaction, just noises."

Joseph's eyes widen. "In your dream?"

"Yeah, I couldn't even see what was going on in my own dream," Michael nods, relenting.

"Wow, that's just... sad." Joseph offers a bewildered shake of his head.

The car rolls on in silence, tires humming against the asphalt, until half a mile down the road, Joseph can no longer contain his amusement and cracks up.

Donnie and Jared slip into a quiet corner of the chaotic backyard party, propping themselves against a white PVC fence. Donnie sips at the beer inside his plastic cup, watching from afar as Lucas cheers on his newfound female friends in some unwritten, drunken contest he doesn't understand.

Donnie nudges Jared, tossing out, "Do you know whose house this is?"

"Nah, I think Louie knows the kid," Jared shrugs, pointing toward his friend. Lucas pours the contents of his cup into the mouth of a kneeling girl, slowly raising it higher and higher. The group cheers, urging them not to let a single drop spill to the floor. Lucas is making quite a name for himself at the party, drawing a crowd with his antics, while the two of them are left to mingle on their own.

"That's cool," Donnie says, sipping his drink and watching the many female partygoers strolling by. He takes another sip, the cup's plastic edge cool against his lips, eyes flicking to the girls, then darting away. He contemplates his almost-empty red cup, trying to muster the guts, or at least down enough liquid courage, to approach one.

"Oh shit, this song is sick!" Donnie's face lights up as he recognizes the pulsating beats of Amber's *Above the Clouds*, heightening the energy among those in attendance. Closed fists pump upward and outward in a semi-circular fashion, loose clothing flying about as people twirl together in time to the music. The fellas in attendance flex the muscles in their arms as they move, mirroring each other like participants in an ancient battle. The ladies showcase their footwork and hip sways, swirling and stepping to the rhythm. The dancing at the party, more than just bodies grinding together, is a chance to show off skills and outshine the rest.

Donnie's head bobs in time to the beat, but Jared, despite his typical enthusiasm, stares out at the distant dancers. "What's wrong with you, dude? You've said two words the whole fucking night: jack and shit," Donnie points out, hitting Jared across the arm with a slap.

Jared tenses at the impact. "Nothing. Alright, I'm bored," Donnie cocks his head toward Jared, clearly not swallowing the bullshit his friend is serving. "It's just that..." But before Jared can finish his thought, a hoot and holler of *"Eat him!"* comes from Lucas's crowd, drawing the duo's attention.

Since they last noticed, Lucas has somehow misplaced his shirt. Their friend stands Christ-like on top of a table, his naked arms outstretched wide. He's joined by the tan blonde, who bites his left shoulder, while the brunette tugs at his right earlobe with her teeth.

"I wonder what that's about? Come on, instead of standing around here like a bunch of fags, let's check it out," Donnie suggests.

Jared grabs his friend's arm, stopping him. "You're gonna cockblock him."

"Better than standing around here holding my dick in my hand all fucking night," Donnie retorts, heading toward the commotion.

Jared shifts on his feet, then trails after Donnie. With each step, his shoulders ease, his stride lightens. Maybe the effort to join in is all it takes to shake away the unease he's been feeling about himself. He walks toward the group in a straight line, not watching where he's going. He accidentally bumps into a girl in a cropped tee. She stumbles, and Jared grabs her arms, stopping her from tumbling to the ground. Her hair tangles from the jerk, but her expression shifts from anger to surprise when she sees the familiar face of her rescuer.

Jared recognizes the face in his arms, noticing the sparkle of recognition in her eyes. His mind blanks, and he can't place her name. "Hey, hey you, how are you?" Jared asks, hugging her to stall for time.

The girl crosses her arms and stares daggers at him. "You remember me?"

"Sure, sure I do," Jared replies, faking confidence, a shit-eating grin forming across his lips.

The girl maintains eye contact and places a well-manicured finger on the top of his chest, a white scratch line trailing as she drags it down to the center of his pecs. "Oh yeah? What's my name?" she challenges.

Jared switches tactics, challenging her back. "Um, let's see. If you tell me mine, I'll tell you yours." His playful charm cuts through his initial panic, leveling the playing field.

"Jared Herschblatt," her response triumphant, her glossy lips shining as she takes her time enunciating every syllable of his name.

"Wow, good. Last name and everything, huh?" He chuckles, caught off guard by her recall while his own falters. "Whew, talk about being put on the spot," he says with a grin.

Forgotten name girl rolls her eyes, glistening lips twitching in annoyance, and turns away. "Catch you later, Hershey-Boy," she exclaims and bounces off.

Donnie slaps his hand down hard onto Jared's shoulder, startling him away from watching the jiggle in the girl's gait. "Oh, that was slick," he laughs into Jared's face. "What happened? She found out you were a fag?"

Jared jerks Donnie's hand off his shoulder and fumes, the sun-kissed freckles on his face suddenly ringed in red. Spittle flies from his mouth, landing on Donnie's cheek. "You know, that's the type of shit that really bothers me. I'm not a fag!"

Hatcher, unaware of the growing tension between the two friends, pushes them both aside, jumping up and down while pointing to the deck overhanging the pool. "Check it out!"

Following Hatcher's gesture, Jared and Donnie's eyes turn upward. Lucas, who had climbed onto the deck's railing moments earlier, now stands there, letting out a yell before plunging into the water.

The crowd erupts in rowdy cheers, fists punching the air, and a few of the more daring souls splash into the pool. Jared squints through the blur of splashing bodies but is positive Lucas has not only misplaced his shirt but also the rest of his clothes.

Soaked girls ride on top of broad shoulders, splashing about as they push each other back down into the water. Donnie and Hatcher buckle over in laughter, amused by Lucas's audacity. Jared, however, remains unmoved by the display. Lucas is always a good time, and he has a natural charm that can't be faked, but these days, he's been getting reckless.

"That kid is insane," Hatcher comments, admiration evident in his voice. Jared stands there, the night's havoc pressing in, thick as the crowd's sweat and laughter. Lucas's smile is bright, but Jared watches him, his brow furrowing as he notices the glossed-over look in his friend's eyes.

The ice cubes clink against the glass as Joseph takes the first sip of his drink. He asked for black, but the bartender handed him a different blend; still, scotch is scotch, and though the initial taste is rough, he's confident his palate will warm to it. Most patrons at the bar are nursing beers, but given the choice, Joseph prefers the harsh, smoky tones of scotch, a taste he picked up from an old Chicagoan friend at MSU. It's also the cocktail his uncles toasted with at weddings. *Scotch is a man's drink.*

Michael secures them a small standing table in a dimly lit corner. The air thick with the scent of spilled beer and old wood, the hum of voices and cigarette smoke wafting around them. Joseph returns with the next round. Lisa had arrived first, waiting outside with a warm smile. Joseph noticed Michael stiffen as she approached for a hug. He offered to buy the first round, knowing the bartender would be slow, giving Michael and Lisa a chance to settle into the night.

"Michael, you never actually introduced me to your cousin," Lisa reminds him as Joseph sets the beers in front of them.

"Oh, this is my cousin, Joseph." Michael shifts his weight, his voice flat. Joseph flashes a small, tight-lipped smile and nods toward Lisa. "Joseph, meet Lisa. We've known each other for years."

Joseph extends his hand to Lisa, and they exchange a formal handshake. "Nice to meet you; Michael speaks highly of you," he says. Their hands linger a beat too long, and he pulls back first, returning to his drink. Lisa's eyes lock with his, but Joseph closes his own, avoiding her gaze. *She's more attractive than he'd anticipated*, and knowing Michael likes her, he drops his eyes, a flush creeping up his neck as her smile lingers in his mind.

"You guys usually hang out together a lot," Joseph says, glancing at Michael before turning to Lisa. "I feel like I'm crashing something."

"No, no, I love *Screaming Broccoli*. They're playing tonight. Usually, there's a bunch of us, but no one else could make it."

Michael points to the speakers and drum kit near the middle of the bar, amps humming with low static. "They're good. Saw them down the shore, didn't even know they played up here until Lisa told me."

Lisa's gaze lingers on Joseph, and his grin falters, uncertain. He glances at Michael, catching his cousin's smile tighten, as if the unease has shifted to him.

"It's nice that you two could just hang out together. I love being around my cousin; he's a fun guy to hang out with," Joseph says, trying to steer the conversation toward Michael.

"Yeah, if you don't mind the sneakers," Michael jokes.

"You are the only one in here with sneakers on," Joseph laughs, shaking his head.

Lisa laughs, her eyes crinkling at the cousins' banter. "It's refreshing to see you guys like to hang out together. I can't stand my cousins." Her hand brushes Joseph's, and he jerks it back, grabbing his glass.

"Cool, uh, yeah, Bella and I go see live music all the time...*my girlfriend,*" he finishes, nodding toward Lisa, answering an unasked question.

Mentioning Bella helps; it lets Lisa know he's spoken for. Not mentioning her feels like denying her, distancing himself.

"She's in Michigan," Michael continues, causing Joseph to choke on his scotch, coughing it back into the glass.

The flicker of disappointment Lisa shows when Joseph mentions Bella vanishes. "Oh, what's she doing there?"

"She lives there," Michael continues, oblivious to Joseph's discomfort. Joseph hits Michael's foot with his own under the table, prompting a loud, "What?" from Michael.

"He means she's at school there. I just graduated; she's a year under me," Joseph clarifies.

"Under you," Lisa echoes, letting the words linger before continuing. "Oh, that's wonderful. It's nice to see someone so committed, even with the long distance."

"Let me tell you, long-distance relationships are like navigating a minefield. They rarely work out in the end," Michael jumps in, tripping over his own words.

Lisa leans forward, revealing a curved line of cleavage, her eyes narrowing with intent. *"Oh, really?* Is that your perspective on things, Michael?"

Joseph's jaw tightens at his cousin's interjection. It feels like Michael is blocking every effort he makes to deflect Lisa's attention. Either he's doing it on purpose, or Michael is just hopelessly unequipped to read the room. Knowing his cousin, Joseph glances at Michael's awkward sway, a wry smile tugging at his lips.

"Yeah, call me a cynic, but distance, man, it takes a special kind of commitment to make it work," Michael continues. Joseph never wanted to smack his cousin across the back of the head more, but he somehow resists, his fingers tightening around the glass.

"We've been together for quite a while, and we have a special commitment," Joseph quickly defends, seizing on Michael's words. "I can't imagine my life without her," he adds, but the band's speakers buzz to life, drowning out his voice.

Joseph, taking a cue from the band, decides to step away. "I'm going to check them out," he announces, grabs his drink, and leaves Michael and Lisa alone at the table.

The area around the band grows crowded, the air thick with sweat and anticipation. The shoulder-to-shoulder crowd bumps and spills, coating the stained wood floor with alcohol. Joseph, having refreshed his glass at the bar, positions himself in the middle of the crowd and breathes a sigh of relief. The scent of body spray and spilled beer mingles with the sound of laughter. It's better to let them have some time together, he thinks. Out of sight, out of mind.

The band launches into an impressive cover of Smashing Pumpkins' *1979*, the crowd roaring in approval. The guitar riffs pulse through the sticky air.

Growing up the son of a musician, Joseph was always more critical of live music than his friends. Even though he wasn't a trained musician himself, it was hard to turn off the critical ear ingrained in him from years of hearing how a band should sound. He hears a slight waver in the singer's pitch and winces, his ear twitching. The scotch helps dull the analytical breakdown in his mind, and he finds himself enjoying the music despite the imperfections.

Joseph brings the scotch to his lips, crunching the last ice cube between his teeth before draining the glass. The brown liquid works its magic, loosening his mood and dulling his senses. He smiles, engulfed in the crowd of strangers. It's been a minute since he's enjoyed himself like this, just feeling the moment without worrying about the future. He's so engrossed in the music that he doesn't notice Lisa until her hand squeezes his arm.

"Hey, there you are," she says, startling him. The music's loud, so she leans in close, her breath hot against his neck. The scent of her perfume stirs a raw thrill inside him.

"Oh, hey, where's Michael?" Joseph blurts out.

Lisa nods toward the corner. "He said he didn't want to lose the table." Joseph looks over and sees Michael standing guard, solo. "Told you they were good, no?" Lisa's voice pulls his attention back.

"Oh yeah, awesome," Joseph agrees.

Lisa stays close, swaying to the music, enjoying the performance as much as Joseph. As the band introduces the next song, his muscles relax, and he starts to sway with the rhythm. Since she approached him, there haven't been any more flirtations; they simply enjoy the show like old friends. Joseph glances at her, then away, wondering if he's misread her intentions. They're just two people in a packed bar, sharing the music.

The band finishes their set, promising to return for a second, and the house DJ drops a pulsing techno beat. The majority of the crowd stays on the floor as the atmosphere shifts from concert to nightclub. Joseph's shoulders loosen as he moves to the beat, Lisa becoming his dance partner. They share smiles and laughs as one song blends into two, and the DJ transitions into reggae.

Lisa pulls Joseph close, pressing her backside against his crotch, moving sensually to the music. Caught off guard but unwilling to break the rhythm, he moves in time with her. His hands hover awkwardly at his sides, hesitating as he considers what it would mean to let them explore her body.

Joseph feels his jeans tighten as Lisa moves deliberately, grinding against him. Her skillful hips lock in and bring him to full attention. Without breaking contact, she arches backward, her hair brushing his shoulder, filling his senses with the spicy warmth of her scent. She turns to face him, their legs intertwining, hips pressing together with no space between. Their eyes lock, desire throbbing in the sliver of air that remains.

"I'm gonna check on Michael," Joseph breaks the contact abruptly and rushes away, nearly slipping on a wet spot beneath him.

Lisa watches him leave, brow furrowed in confusion. She resumes dancing, blending back into the pulsating crowd as if the moment never happened. Joseph reaches Michael, immediately chastising him, "What's wrong with you? Get out there."

"I don't want to lose the table."

"Fuck the table, I got the table, I know you like that girl." Come hell or high water, Joseph is staying away from Lisa. Maybe if he pushes Michael hard enough, he'd find his own balls and act.

Michael's eyebrows shoot up in surprise, and he gives Joseph a warning look. "Come on, Joe."

"No, no, I'm serious! Michael, you're a great guy, you're funny," Joseph rolls his eyes, tossing in a small tease. "Okay, sometimes you're funny, but she's all teed up, and she'd be lucky to have you."

Joseph braces for a self-deprecating remark from his cousin. Instead, he's pleasantly surprised as Michael takes his advice, leaves the comfort of the table, and joins Lisa on the dance floor.

Joseph watches as Michael's hips sway out of time with the bass-heavy beats. Lisa leans into him, appreciating the effort. His eyes widen as she takes his hand, guiding him to the rhythm. The two look happy together, and Lisa's smirk tells Joseph he's done the right thing.

Joseph enjoys seeing the smile form on Michael's lips and hopes his sloppy matchmaking pays off. He exhales, shoulders easing as he watches them. He isn't sure how much Michael saw when he was dancing with Lisa, but he's glad it only went so far.

When they were on the floor together, it was easy to imagine their dance continuing under the covers. The thought itself made him feel like he was betraying Michael's trust and cheating on Bella. As the night wears on, he asks himself which feeling guided his actions: the fear of facing his cousin or the guilt of lusting after another woman while committed to Bella?

The room lies still, black-and-white images of Ralph Kramden and his wife Alice flickering across the television screen. Ralph's booming voice breaks the silence: "Baby, you're the greatest!" Polite applause from the TV audience stirs Anthony from his slumber. Groggily, he shifts on the couch, caught in a fog of sleep, then tumbles onto the floor with a soft thud, fully awake.

Anthony rubs his eyes, yawns, and grapples with his bearings. The television's dim glow casts long, eerie shadows across the furniture, bathing the room in a ghostly light. He scans the surroundings, taking in the familiar decor, the worn armchair, the faded curtains, and the slumbering figures of Angela, Ezra, and Jackie sprawled across the couch. The lingering scent of popcorn hangs in the air, a faint reminder of their earlier snack, now cold and forgotten.

His eyes shift to the clock, the second hand unrelenting as it ticks toward the future, accenting the demise of any prior evening plans. A pang of disappointment hits him, another night slipping away. Anthony nudges Jackie softly, his touch gentle as he encourages her to awaken.

"Jackie, wake up," he whispers, his voice soft but tinged with disappointment. "It's late."

"What's going on?" she mumbles, her voice thick with sleep.

Roused by her cousin's voice, Angela stirs from her slumber, her face mirroring his confusion as she slowly opens her eyes. Anthony, unwilling to let the night end, lets his mind race. An idea sparks. "I'm hungry," he declares. "I'm going to walk with Jackie to the diner."

Angela's eyes narrow at the still-sleeping Ezra, a spark of intrigue flickering across her face. Her eyebrows tilt in disappointment as he remains lost in sleep, the faint sounds of snores purring from his nose. Unlike Anthony's gentle nudge, Angela rears back and punches Ezra hard on the shoulder.

"Come on," she commands. "We're going to the diner, then you're driving my cousin home."

Ezra springs awake, eyes bulging, fists clenching from the shock. "What? What time is it?"

"I'm telling you that girl likes you," Joseph insists, his voice edged with excitement.

"And I'm telling you *that girl likes you*," Michael replies, chuckling.

The car rolls to a stop, and Michael shifts it into park. Joseph pauses before exiting, his face clouding with thought.

"You know, you shouldn't be so hard on yourself. At least you have friends to call up and girls to hang out with," Joseph turns away from his cousin, taking in the house he grew up in. "Sometimes, I wish my life was like that again. If it weren't for Bella, I'd have nobody to talk to."

Michael's eyebrows shoot up, his mouth opening slightly as he processes Joseph's words. His cousin Joseph has the girl, the college degree, the looks, and though Michael is technically taller, Joseph always seems to rise above. "What? Are you saying you envy me?"

Joseph shrugs. "Sure, why not?"

"Score one for the most negative man alive," Michael says, a rare smile crossing his face as he takes the compliment.

"Whatever, I'm going to bed," Joseph says, smacking his cousin on the shoulder and winking as he gets out of the car. He reaches his front door, and as the living room light spills into the night, Michael drives off.

Lost in thought, Joseph climbs the staircase. He enters the cluttered, cramped bedroom he shares with his two brothers. Anthony is already sound asleep. His gaze shifts to Lucas's bed, still empty. Exhaustion courses through his body, and without changing out of his clothes, Joseph collapses onto his mattress and surrenders to sleep's embrace.

The Nissan's front tire slams against the curb, jolting the car to a stop at an awkward angle. The engine cuts off, and Lucas stumbles out of the driver's side door, the stench of alcohol trailing behind him. He lurches toward the front door, only to jump as the screen door slams shut with a bang. Lucas spins around, finger to his lips, hissing, *"Shhhh."* He glances over his shoulder and, with exaggerated care, eases the front door closed as quietly as his drunken state allows. Satisfied, he weaves through the dark living room but trips over Joseph's scattered college remnants. Fists clenched, irritation boiling over, he abandons stealth and kicks over some of his brother's belongings.

Lucas tosses his shoes into the corner of the nearby foyer closet. He removes his shirt, glances at his reflection in a nearby mirror, and flexes his muscles. He sways, staring at the multiple reflections staring back at him. He shakes away the blurry distortion and makes his way upstairs to his bedroom.

His gaze falls upon his slumbering brothers, and he collapses onto his bed. Uncomfortable and without blankets, Lucas curls up, trying to find warmth within his body heat. The rhythmic snores grate on his nerves. His brain swims in a mix of cranberry juice, vodka, and beer. The snoring amplifies to *a thousand decibels* in his head. He twists his pillow over his face and ears, pulling his knees in tighter against his chest. As if in response to his attempts to muffle them, the snores become as loud as a rock concert. Annoyed, he stares at the ceiling and lets out a frustrated groan into the pillow, his voice hoarse with exasperation.

Lucas lifts the pillow from his ears and smacks Joseph across the face with it. For a few seconds, the snoring ceases, granting him a sense of tranquility. Content, Lucas curls up once again, hoping the nightmare is over and he can enjoy a peaceful night's rest. Yet, to his dismay, the snoring resumes, its steady rhythm reverberating through the room. Lucas springs out of bed and, in an act of irritation, delivers a swift kick to Anthony's mattress. He paces down the hall, seeking solace, and collapses into the bathtub for temporary refuge.

The cold, hard metal of the tub quickly loses whatever comfort it once offered, and Lucas decides to return to his bedroom. Instead of lying back down, he grabs his pillow and snatches a blanket off Joseph. Quickly exiting, he makes his way downstairs. He tumbles the pillow and blanket down in front of him, retrieving them once his trek to the basement is complete. Lucas arranges the items on the couch, sloppily assembling a makeshift bed. Weary from the events of the night, Lucas settles onto the couch and seeks solace in the quiet darkness of the basement. Eventually, sleep claims him, and he surrenders to the embrace of a black, dreamless slumber.

"Because you had to be a big shot, didn't you
You had to open up your mouth
You had to be a big shot, didn't you
All your friends were so knocked out"
-Billy Joel

NINE

BIG SHOT

The insistent buzz of Frisco's alarm clock violently jerks him awake from his troubled slumber. He groans, extending his arm to silence the blaring noise. His jaw clenches, eyes narrowing as he takes in the obsessively neat bedroom. His chest tightens like a vise as he sits up, fingers trembling slightly. He inhales the room's stale, dust-free air and exhales with an audible whoosh. Yielding to the daylight filtering through his curtains, he leaps from the mattress, folds the covers over his pillows with military precision, and aligns the comforter along its edges and corners.

The knocking on the door arrives earlier than usual, but his mother's voice remains muffled by the wooden barrier.

"I'm up, I'm up!" Frisco yells, silencing the persistent knocks.

His hand levels a lone plaque on the wall, fingers lingering over the laminated news article inside, along with the black-and-white smile of his younger self. "Giuseppe Friscaldino scores three goals in one game to lead his team to the playoffs."

He shuffles his feet into black Nike sandals, grabs the handle of his bedroom door, and slowly pushes it ajar. His mother's muffled voice drifts from down the hall, no doubt waking Gary more gently. His brother is only three years younger, but she babies the boy. She's been different since his father left them, and Frisco takes the brunt of it. The oldest man in the house now with the same name as the one who hurt her. It's unfair. He clenches at the thought of how differently she treats them, but he loves her anyway. How could he not? She is, after all, his mother.

Frisco quickly scuttles into the sanctuary of the bathroom, locking the door behind him. His mother is quick to notice, the bathroom door becoming her new punching bag. The pounding cuts through him as he twists on the shower. Water cascades down, steam beading on the pristine white subway tile. The soothing hiss of the shower holds no effect against the shrill ferocity of his mother's voice.

"Giuseppe! Giuseppe! There are other people in this house!" she bellows.

Standing naked under the showerhead, Frisco imagines closing his eyes would equate to closing his ears. The shower should serve as a place of rejuvenation, but her implied demands shatter the brief calm. They pierce through the relaxation, birthing fresh butterflies in his guts.

Frisco takes a deep breath, trying to steady his voice before answering. "Alright, Ma! I'm getting out already!" He hopes the water, steam, and door will conceal the anger in his voice.

He lathers quickly, rinses even faster, and wraps a towel securely around his waist. Still dripping with water from his hurried shower, he emerges from the bathroom, greeted by his mother with her arms crossed and face stern.

"Are you going to clean your room today?" she demands, her voice sharp.

Unlike the hearty chuckles he shares with friends and strangers, the laugh that echoes down the hallway is a joyless roar.

"You mind if I get dressed first?" His gaze meets hers, hard as steel.

"Don't start, Giuseppe. I've been telling you for a week to clean that room," her gaze briefly shifts away.

Frisco brushes past her, his movements brusque and devoid of playfulness. Returning to his bedroom, he slams the door shut with force, causing the pictures on the hallway wall to rattle, shaking the fractured memories of a family that has long lost its harmony.

T he glossy purple bowling ball slams into the left side of the dull white headpin with a booming crack, the pins clattering like a sudden downpour. Frisco stands with his eyes fixed on the lone pin wobbling in the corner, waiting for it to decide whether to stand or fall. It succumbs to the momentum of the sway and joins its brothers on the ground before being swept clear by the large mechanical arm. It was a cheap Jersey strike, as Staten Islanders would call it, the ball missing the pocket but landing with enough force on the other side of the headpin to carry the rest away with it. Nevertheless, it's marked as an X for scoring purposes all the same.

Frisco adds a little hop to his step, grimacing as he claps his hands together, the right hand slicing down hard across the left. He turns to John, who's watching with a grin.

"Looks like you let that one hang a little," John says.

Frisco pulls him into a warm hug. "Hey John, how you doing?"

"Good, good. How's your game going?"

Frisco sighs, "Miserable. Can't find the pocket or finish a spare. Without those lucky Jersey strikes, I'd be struggling. But hey, I'm just here for fun."

John chuckles, shaking his head at Frisco's feigned nonchalance. "You're always here, man. Don't you have any other hobbies?"

Frisco grins, "Well, I play soccer too. Scored three goals in a single game once, led my team to the playoffs. I'm practically a Staten Island icon."

Pins crashed and balls thudded around them as the pair shared a laugh, Billy Joel's voice crackling warmly from the alley's old speakers. John watches Frisco's form as he approaches the line and smoothly releases the ball onto the well-oiled pine. The sixteen-pound ball gathers speed, its glossy surface picking up streaks of oil off the lane. It crosses over a dot, then an arrow, before hooking back toward the red-necked headpin.

"On the Over!" Frisco hollers.

Frisco sits surrounded by some of his favorite Vitagliano women. Grandma's lace-covered dining table isn't as full as it normally is on a Sunday, but it still holds enough sweets, crumb cake, and rainbow cookies to keep company in place. Angela, still in her dirt-streaked softball uniform, snatches a rainbow cookie while Sofia leans back, listening intently. Frisco's hands dance in the air, his face a canvas of exaggerated expressions. The women burst into laughter, their faces bright with amusement as he engages them in story. Grandma serves him a piece of crumb cake. He flashes a greedy smile without missing a beat, then leans forward, his voice animated as he continues regaling the ladies.

"So I turn around and say, Look, if you're the shit and I'm the shit, why don't we get together and make a big stink?"

"Stop," Aunt Cici says, bubbling up as she laughs and slaps his shoulder. "When did this happen?"

"At Danielle's wedding. I think she has it on the tape," Frisco grins, recalling the event. "Stella couldn't stop laughing, you know, a typical response to me from you Vitagliano girls."

"Don't worry, Frisco," Angela teases, her voice quick and light, nodding toward Aunt Cici's new granddaughter. "You still have a shot at getting into the family. There's always Naomi."

"Forget Naomi, Angela. *I want you,*" Frisco reaches out for Angela. She squirms away as if his touch were a hot iron, her lips twisting sideways and her tongue recoiling at the thought.

Sofia laughs at her sister's over-the-top reaction, and Frisco turns his attention her way. "I was only saying that to make you jealous, baby."

"Oh yeah, right, like I would ever," Sofia shoots back, dismissing the idea with a click of her hand, her distaste mirroring Angela's.

His laughter ripples through the table, and soon they all join in on the fun. Frisco's chest warms as he regards them, their voices wrapping him like a familiar blanket.

"Coffee?" Grandma calls from the kitchen.

Frisco shakes his head no. "Grandma, you won't believe what happened to me once."

Angela and Sofia roll their eyes so hard you'd swear they groan aloud. "He scored three goals in one game to lead his team to the playoffs," they chime in unison, cutting off Frisco's glory before he can finish.

"Oh, I'm sorry. You know, unlike some families, not to mention any names, normal people usually aren't in the paper every week," Frisco says, a grin tugging at his lips.

The laughter swells, washing away any hint of sting. Frisco takes the teasing in stride, his smile deepening. He knows it's their way of showing love, a stark contrast to the brittle tension he feels with his brother. Gary is too soft for it; he'd bristle at every jab. Here, among the Vitagliano women, Frisco savors the relentless banter and the threads of affection behind the ball-busting.

"Oh, where's Louie?" Angela asks.

"I was headed over there before I decided to pop in. I better get going," Frisco rises, making sure to kiss each of their cheeks goodbye, the gesture tender and familiar. As he steps out, the laughter trails after him, a soft echo of family and home.

The green felt is worn thin from years of abuse, marred by faded drink stains, smudged blue chalk, and jagged black tears scattered across the playing surface. The cue stick glides through Joseph's fingers. With a sharp crack, he strikes the matte white ball dead center, breaking the rack apart in a burst of color.

Frisco awaits his turn, holding the pool cue like a staff and leaning on it as he watches himself on the television.

"This is it; here's where your brother gives the assist," Frisco points the edge of the cue toward the television. A shaky, taped high school soccer game crackles on the old TV.

In near unison, the cue ball drops into the side pocket just as the Frisco on the television screen strikes the soccer ball into the net.

"Yep, look how great I am! *Three goals*, three goals. I get choked up every time," Frisco turns from the screen and spots Joseph leaning against the billiard table, the wall of golden trophies earned by the Vitaglianos looming over his shoulder. Joseph's face stays blank, giving nothing away.

"Scratch, you're up," Joseph informs Frisco.

Frisco arrived unannounced. Lucas isn't home, but Frisco came over anyway. He makes himself at home, gliding comfortably into the house, the fridge opening for him without hesitation. The bread, utensils, and microwave are all familiar, as are his movements around the kitchen, clearly a dance he's performed many times.

Joseph was grateful he'd thrown on shorts and a T-shirt for the day, instead of the usual stained tank top and clashing boxers. A knock at the back door caught him off guard, announcing Frisco's arrival. Frisco wasn't interrupting anything important, maybe some N64 time or another crack at the resume, but there were no solid plans for the day in place. Nevertheless, he wished for a quieter afternoon.

Joseph had never hung out unaccompanied with the kid and wasn't sure how to pass the time. He isn't sure whose idea it was to play pool, but they racked them up just the same. At some point during Frisco's lopsided, nonstop monologuing – spilling out like an overturned bucket – he loaded a videotape to showcase his athletic prowess.

"So, have you talked to your sister lately?" Frisco pivots from the TV and lines up the cue ball.

"No, but she'll be home soon," Joseph answers, watching Frisco measure his shot and chalk his cue. Joseph isn't sure what to make of this kid who spends nearly every waking hour in his parents' house. Frisco uncorks where Lucas clams shut. He spills details Lucas keeps locked, a deluge of nonsense, silly adventures, inside jokes, how high school ended, and how college has been treating them.

But then the words strike Joseph, sharp as the clack of the billiard balls bouncing off each other. "Yeah, that chick spun his head around, off to the races ever since. Just notches on your couch over there." Frisco's spilling about Lucas and a recent breakup. *Holy shit!* Joseph's grip tightens on his cue, his thoughts scatter, and Frisco's stepping too far. This isn't his to share. Lucas will be pissed if he hears it got out.

Lucas loves, apparently; Lucas did love; and Lucas could also be broken by love.

It clears up some things for Joseph: his brother's edge, his sharp bite, his general dickishness. Still, you have to consider the source. Joseph narrows his eyes, weighing Frisco's words. Not everything coming out of his mouth is gospel. Worse, he's now asking about his sister. The whole vibe feels off.

"She had to finish a summer credit to complete her degree. And, um, she's bringing her boyfriend to live with us," Joseph adds, his tone flat.

Frisco sends the cue ball rolling across the felt. It strikes the maroon seven, sinking it firmly into the left corner pocket. Frisco circles the table, his eyes widening, a smirk tugging at his lips. "Oh my, now that should be interesting. Seven of you in this house? Forget about it! If you thought I was over here a lot now, I'm going to permanently glue my ass to the couch just to watch the fireworks."

Frisco takes his second shot. The cue ball glances off the purple four and positions itself perfectly behind the striped yellow nine. Not sinking any solids, he hands over the table to Joseph. "Where did your brother go?" Frisco asks as Joseph calculates the possible angles.

"Well, Tony is at Jackie's," Joseph replies, "And I think Lucas went to pick up Hatcher."

Speak of the devil and you'll hear the flutter of his wings. With an entrance timed to perfection, Lucas slides open the basement door.

"Oh hey, what's up?" he calls out to Frisco, ignoring his brother. "Do you have something to swim in? We're going to play a little pool basketball."

"Pool basketball? Are we going to use Vitagliano rules or try to play a game that someone not named Vitagliano can win?" Frisco follows Lucas out, exiting into the blinding glare of a sunny day. Joseph remains behind in the harsh fluorescent glow of the basement. He strikes the cue ball, the clink echoing in the emptiness, as it sinks the striped nine ball into the pocket.

Angie startles herself with the intensity of her scream. A jolt of shock ripples through her, melting into disbelief. Her eyes are awash with bright yellow as her baby boy stands before her. The jet-black hair Angie and Anthony used to share? Gone. Replaced by a garish platinum headful of bleach-blond hair.

"So, how do you like it?" Anthony asks, a smile almost as bright as his dome flashing across his face.

Angie lets loose another scream, this one more playful than the last. Anthony laughs at her reaction, enjoying the chaos his cosmetic change has unleashed.

"What's the matter? What's going on?" Joseph rushes into the kitchen, sliding on the tiles and nearly crashing into his brother.

Angie, struggling to speak, points at Anthony. "What did you do!?"

Joseph's limbs go limp. He realizes there's no danger, just his brother's ridiculous new hairstyle. Slightly shaky from hearing his mother's screams, he relaxes, grasping what all the fuss is about.

"I can't seem to get a good look," Joseph says as he squints his eyes, staring directly into his brother's golden locks. "Tony, maybe if you turned down the volume of your head, I might see a little better." He perks up, a thought igniting. "Wait, wait," he slides open a nearby drawer, rummages for a moment, and pulls out a pair of sunglasses.

"Nope, still too bright," Joseph quips, placing the shades on his face.

"Jackie's mom did it," Anthony answers the unasked question.

Joseph places his hands on the sides of his face. "Tony, just stand right there. Ahhh, I can get a tan off it."

"I thought you said you were just going to do highlights," Angie says, her voice cracking.

"Yeah, but I kinda like it like this," Anthony's smile beams brighter.

Joseph drapes an arm around his stunned mother's shoulder, consoling her. "Ma, look on the bright side. It will keep him safe when jogging at night."

"Daddy's gonna be mad, huh?" Anthony asks, his smile starting to fade with worry.

Angie's lips part, then press tight, no words escaping. "It's just so *blonde*!" Unable to say any more, she directs her son toward the kitchen balcony. "Go outside, show your brother."

Drawn by the distant shouts and splashes, Anthony goes out onto the balcony. The pool basketball game is in full swing; Lucas and his boys continue their play, oblivious to Anthony's transformation. Anthony leans against the railing, his eyes alight at the chaos below. Lucas, Frisco, Jared, and Hatcher engage in a rough game, splashing water like fountains and churning it with underwater wrestling. The basketball net wobbles next to the pool's vinyl walls, swaying with each rough shove.

Lucas, his relentless drive flaring up even in a casual game, dunks Jared's head underwater. He leaps over him, trying to swipe the ball from Frisco's grasp. His aim goes awry, delivering a stinging slap to Frisco's face and nose. Frisco lets out a scream that echoes through the backyard. Hatcher grabs the ball and aims for a shot but stops short, noticing Anthony watching from above.

"Oh my God! Look at your brother," Hatcher exclaims.

Anthony descends from the upper deck. He approaches the pool, readying himself for the inevitable comments about to come his way.

"Pret-ty, so pret-ty," Frisco chimes in first.

"What the hell? Did Jackie get tired of looking at you the other way?" Lucas teases.

"No. I wanted to do it," Anthony says.

"I think it looks good," Jared offers, earning glances of disapproval from the waterlogged crew.

"You coming in the pool, or do you have enough chemicals in your hair?" Lucas splashes a wave of chlorinated water at him.

Anthony jumps back, dodging it. "Besides, when it grows out, it'll look phat."

"Okay, Antoinette, or should I call you Mr. Jackie?" Lucas continues, deepening his voice on Jackie's name.

Anthony shrugs off the hair jabs; he dishes out the disses with the best of them. But Lucas's relentless digs about Jackie wear thin. A switch flips on his teenage temper, and his joy ignites to anger. "Shut up. What's your problem anyway? Oh yeah, I forgot, your friends are around, so you have to act all cool."

"At least I have friends, unlike some people who forget about them to hang out with his girlfriend all the time."

The words come faster now; Anthony is done with Lucas's taunts. "Just wait. I can't wait till you meet somebody else you really like. I can't wait."

"Yeah, well, I wouldn't forget about my friends or my family," Lucas digs in harder. Sooner or later, Anthony needs to learn what matters, and it isn't loyalty to some broad.

Anthony's fists tighten; he's done arguing with his jerk-off brother. He turns his back on the pool and storms off.

Lucas steams, his face twisting; his protective glare morphs into a scowl. He jumps out of the pool, grabs a nearby garden hose, and aims it at his fleeing brother. A frigid jet of water blasts out, catching Anthony's sneakers as he double-times up the deck's stairs. Lucas follows his retreat with the hose, continuing to spray even as Anthony slips back from the railings and into the kitchen. The water pounds the sliding glass door like a storm until Lucas relents.

Angie slides open the door, daggers in her eyes, daring her middle son. "Cut it out!" It's all well and good for her boys to have it out now and then - raising three, she knows it's just part of the deal - but soaking her kitchen pushes too far.

Lucas flashes a crooked smile, the kind he knows melts her resolve. His face shifts from self-righteous teen to the puppy-eyed child she raised. "What? What did I do?"

Anthony, well aware of his brother's tricks and their pull on their mother, shakes his head, refusing to let Lucas win. He rushes over and reappears in the doorway next to her. "You know what? You are such an asshole. Why don't you leave? Nobody wants you here. All you do is start fights!"

Lucas drops any mask of innocence. "At least I'm around to start them, not whipped like you," he retorts. "I bet you ask Jackie for permission before you take a shit."

Anthony tries to charge out of the kitchen. Joseph grabs his shoulder, stopping him on the balcony. Anthony pushes Joseph's hand away and leans over the wooden railing. "Don't even. I didn't forget about what that girl did to you. All you did was stay in bed for a week."

Joseph draws back, thoughts crashing through his head. Anthony's outburst splays out before them all. It solidifies a suspicion Joseph isn't sure of; Frisco told the truth. His brother got dumped, and while it might explain some of his actions this summer, it doesn't excuse all of them.

The once-rowdy pool falls silent. No waves splash; the water remains glassy and still around the boys. Lucas, not willing to appear weak in front of his friends, smiles in defiance. "What's that? My sister Antoinette? I can't hear you. Your hair is too loud."

Anthony leans harder over the railing, his knuckles whitening as he grips it. "Ooh, Mr. Cool. What's the matter? Can't deal with it because your friends are around?"

Lucas laughs, looking around at his crew. "What? I'm sorry, Antoinette, I still can't hear you."

Anthony lets go of the railing, rushing past Joseph and back into the house. Joseph peers over the railing. Lucas, all smiles, splashes a face full of water into Frisco, looking mighty pleased with himself.

Joseph softens his voice, coaxing peace. "Hey, Lou, why don't you cut it out, alright?"

"You should talk. I hear you on the phone with Bella." Lucas jumps out of the pool and grabs the basketball.

Joseph's mouth drops open, caught off guard by how quickly Lucas twists the conversation toward his girl-friend. "What the hell does that have to do with any-thing?"

"You sound like a baby." He pump fakes throwing the ball, but Joseph doesn't flinch.

"You're right, we do. We do that, so what?" Joseph keeps his tone even. Lucas is right, so there's nothing to be gained by denying it. Sure, Joseph might sound foolish to an out-sider, but putting on cutesy voices and calling Bella by little pet names when they talked is fine by him. It's their thing, and it's nothing to be ashamed of.

Anthony bolts from the kitchen, down to the basement, and into the closet.

Among the photo albums, forgotten memorabilia, childhood toys, and duffel bags, he grabs a baseball bat. He exits through the basement doors and charges toward his brother. He swings the metal bat, the air whistling, but misses as Lucas jumps back. Lucas dives into the pool, confident that the water and his friends will keep him safe.

"I wish you would drop dead," Anthony seethes, hissing the words through the gaps in his teeth.

Joseph races down from the balcony, hoping to stop things before someone gets hurt. Lucas's friends fall silent as they watch the familial squabble. They swim away from his side.

"Anthony!" Joseph shouts.

Anthony rears back, his arm arching high, and hurls the metal club toward Lucas. It flies mere centimeters from Lucas's cheek and splashes safely behind him.

"Missed me!" Lucas taunts his now empty-handed sibling.

Anthony charges toward the pool, spying the boombox. He snatches up the radio and raises it over his head. Lucas locks eyes with him, daring him to toss it into the pool.

"Say something now, bitch," Anthony spits.

Joseph grabs the radio's handle, but Anthony refuses to let go, his arms jerking with the pull. "Tony, stop."

"Do it, I don't care. Come on," Lucas rises as much as he can, his stomach breaking the surface as he flexes his chest in provocation.

"Tony, don't. It's not worth it," Joseph lets go of the radio and plants himself in front of Anthony, blocking his view of Lucas. Anthony's grip on the radio loosens, his gaze softening as he meets Joseph's. "Besides, that's my radio."

Joseph notices a fleeting smile on Anthony's face, but it vanishes as he lowers the radio and hands it over. Anthony's fingers linger for a moment before he reluctantly lets go. "I just hate him. He's such a jerk."

Joseph pulls Anthony aside, away from Lucas. "He's just going through something right now; he was hurt badly, you know?" Joseph watches Anthony's reaction. He isn't sure he should even mention Lucas's breakup; he just found out about it himself. But the pain it caused his brother is evident in the reflection he catches in Anthony's eyes. He'll have to ask Lucas about it later; *that's what older brothers are for, right?* For now, the more immediate task is to calm down his youngest brother. "Well, it made him into an asshole. How do you think you would be if Jackie broke up with you?" *Or Bella with me,* Joseph thinks but doesn't share. It's a cruel enough idea; the sound of it doesn't need to be birthed into the universe.

Anthony's adrenaline stops surging, and his body slumps from the absence. Joseph watches his younger brother trudge back into the basement and grab the phone. More than the color of his hair, Joseph sees it now. Anthony has changed. He knows his brother is growing up, and looking hard into his eyes, searching for the little boy he once knew, Joseph grasps that Anthony isn't a baby anymore.

TEN

NIGHTSWIMMING

The sharp tang of fresh paint bites the air in his sister's room, a pungent veil Joseph endures for the sake of privacy. It's an on-and-off project, primarily off, that he's been roped into helping his parents finish. They've been redoing and reorganizing this space since before he returned home. Anthony claimed the room in the years Joseph and Stella were away, his childish scrawl tarnishing the walls with all sorts of silly stick figures, doodles, and superheroes with impossibly skewed limbs. The house had space enough for the two boys to have their own rooms, but with Joseph's return and their elder sister's intermittent arrival looming, they've crammed together again. This bedroom, half-finished, needs to be ready. A task that should've taken a weekend has stretched across the summer, and now a two-week deadline presses close, heavy as the fumes.

Joseph laid the second coat of beige paint an hour ago. He shuts the door, sealing himself in, and settles by the small open window. Leaning into the breeze, he lets the rhythmic chirping of birds pull him into a quiet reverie. The silence wraps around him as the paint dries, thick and slow. Soon, he'll peel away the plastic sheets shrouding the furniture lumped in the room's center and nudge each piece back into place. But a gentle wind, threaded with the faint scent of freshly cut grass, slips through the screen, and his plans dissolve into the endless blue sky.

His thoughts drift to Michigan State. What's the sky like there today? Cloudy? Rain-slicked? Or as breezy and calm as Staten Island?

Three phone lines thread through the house: one in the kitchen, one in the basement, and one here, in Stella's room. A luxury his sister savors, a nod to her status as the only daughter among three younger brothers. His parents call it a girl's privilege. The phone jack, swathed in blue tape, hugs the wall; the phone itself rests on the dresser, draped in plastic. Joseph rises, retrieves it, and peels the tape free. He feeds the clear wire into the jack's square slot. The dial tone hums alive, and with a practiced rhythm, he presses the keys, listens to the ringing, and waits for her voice.

It spills through, silky, soft, laced with that Michigan drawl, and his pulse stumbles faster; a balm against the dull ache he's carried too long.

"Deh-doh baby, how's my silly bear?" Joseph's laugh dips into playful, babyish tones. Lucas might be an asshole, but he's sharp and nailed that one dead-on.

"What have you been up to? How was your day?" He shifts, the initial spark fading as he waits. He craves Bella's voice when they're apart, but now, connected, words slip through his fingers, the conversation thinning like smoke.

"When did this happen? Monday, yeah," Monday feels like a lifetime ago, almost a week swallowed by time. Summer's fading fast, its last breaths hanging on the line. "No, I don't know. Why?"

It was the phone, he thinks. He's never been comfortable with this; too much gets lost without a gesture, a raised brow. *They absolutely need to see each other. It'll smooth out.* "So, when do you think I can come out to visit?" The urge to hop on a plane tomorrow burns fierce. The second Bella gives the green light, he'll make it happen. There's still a sliver of time before her semester starts, plenty enough for a quick trip. He can see it: surprising her at the doorstep, her face lighting up, the kind of joy worth every cent of the ticket. If he had a job, he'd fake a cough, call in sick. As things are now, calling out from lounging around his parents' house isn't going to cause an issue.

"A month! Of course I'm disappointed. I want to see you," His voice tightens, more than want; a restless hunger gnaws at him, sharp and growing. "Are you going to be able to get out here anytime?" An unreasonable request, he knows. Beyond holidays and breaks aside, her college schedule is a beast he remembers too well. Still, he clings to hope. "That's bullshit! Don't worry about the money, I have enough," A plea, a bargain, a lie. "Look, I just miss you a lot. I love you."

The room thickens, paint fumes curling harsh and acrid. The breeze dies, the locked door caging a stillness that traps time itself. Dust motes freeze mid-dance, pinpricks of light falling off them near the plastic-draped furniture. Outside, the world hushes.

"You what? Come on, you can say it," *Love* is their ritual, a call and response stitched into their talks. One says it, the other echoes. More than words, it's a tether, a heartbeat in the gaps. He's so used to it capping their calls he once blurted it to the pizza guy after ordering a pie.

"Why? Is there anyone around?" The question sours the moment it's out, cheap, petty, and regret stings sharp. "Jeez, Bella, I'm not commanding you. What kind of nonsense is that? I can't ask my girlfriend to tell me 'I love you'?" Some thoughts should stay buried, he realizes. Spoken, they cut too deep. You can't ask for someone to respect you; they either do or they don't. You can't ask for someone to be sorry; they are either remorseful or they're not. And most importantly, the capo di tutti capi, you can't ask someone to tell you they love you; *they either do or they don't.*

"Fine, don't say it." Silence stretches, taut. "Yeah, whatever."

His words spill fast, "Mad? No, why would I be mad? A little upset, yeah." His voice bounces off the bare walls, sharp and strange, climbing louder. An edge he thought he'd dulled slices through him, raw and alive.

"Well, first, it's like my girlfriend doesn't even want to see me; then she can't even say 'I love you.'" A sudden knock jolts him. His head snaps toward it, but Bella's faint murmur pulls him back. He lets the sound fade unanswered.

"What? What do you mean you have to go?" His voice cracks, disbelief splintering it. "I just got on the phone with you. This is a real bonus to what I was just saying." The walls gleam, slick with fresh paint, a crisp, cool beige he clings to. The furniture, a shapeless heap, grates on him.

He can't deal with the sight of it and turns away, tracing the smooth sweep of color instead.

"Bella, look, I know you're busy." His fingers tighten around the phone. "But I talk to you like what? Once a week?" Another knock, insistent, ignored. "I don't know what I want to say; I just want to be on the phone with you. Okay." Above, the ceiling stares down, dull and untouched, its off-white gaze unsoftened by paint. It hangs there, imperfect, forgotten.

"Come on, alright, I'll talk about something. Let me think." Why is it so hard? A million absurd thoughts bubble under the surface, waiting to be shared. Any other day, any other time, it's easy, but not now. For now, his mind is coated beige.

"Good, take a break; you need to relax." Another knock. "What do you mean? From us? You need a break from a kid seven hundred miles away calling once a week!" His mother's muffled voice cuts through, something about the closet, his sister's clothes. Bella's tone softens, finally spilling something real, but it slips past him.

"I am listening to you. Do you know how much *not* sense you are making? Please, don't do this." *Why are the walls closer? Why is the knock louder?* "A month! Bella, if you do this, it's over." His mother's pounding cascades, bouncing off the shrinking walls. "Bella, if you need a break from the way our situation is, it's breakup." There it is, the itch that breaks the skin, words dragging like sandpaper across his heart.

The relentless banging yanks his focus. He cups the receiver and screams, "Give me a goddamn minute!" His voice trembles, matching the rumbles in his stomach, as he uncovers the phone and whispers, "Hold on, please, don't go anywhere."

He sets the receiver down and yanks open the door mid-rant. "Fine, make sure your sister's closet is empty on your own. The way you talk to me, wait till I tell your father." His mother's gaze slides past him, her annoyance blazing, the only message she's sending.

Joseph shuts her out, and Angie, who hates locked doors in her house, doesn't enjoy being ignored. "Enough, Ma. Alright, I can't." Joseph yells, meeting his mother's eyes, catching raw hurt flicker there. He isn't used to seeing pain on her face. Her frustration he can shrug off, even disappointment; there's some guilt, but no real problem. But pain? That's rare. His angry shout hurt her, and shame twists inside him. The door's already ajar, so he might as well swing it all the way open. "My girlfriend's breaking up with me."

Her face shifts, pain melting into sadness for him. She sees her little boy, knee scraped, not a man. Angie wishes it were that simple, fixable with some hydrogen peroxide and a bandage. But nothing in her medicine cabinet is made to mend a breaking heart. "Oh, why?"

No tears, not now. *It's not over yet. There's still time to salvage it,* Joseph thinks. "I don't know," he says, glimpsing a flash of yellow hair ducking into the bathroom. Angie eases the door shut, leaving him in the room, abandoned. There are no kisses to heal this boo-boo, but there are other ways; there is food, and there is tea.

The room transforms again, stretching improbably long. The corner where the phone lies a distant shore. Each step drags anxiety, dread, and embarrassment in its wake. His stomach knots. *Maybe she hung up. Maybe it's done.* He concentrates, listening for the bleating tones of a dead line. But there isn't one, and Joseph wonders if it might've been easier if there were.

"Hello? Okay, good, you're still there." In every relationship, struggles happen, and while Bella could be mean, she's not cruel. "I don't know, I was hoping, you know, you wouldn't hang up." *Now, who's being cruel?*

"I do know you, but you have to admit these last few moments have been weird." Strangely, now that there's something to discuss, Joseph feels a flicker of hope. Perhaps he's overreacting. The anger fades from his voice, and the conversation feels less strained. He curses himself for being stupid; it's all his insecurities, the results of a fucked-up lonely summer. *It's all going to be okay,* he's sure of it.

And then he hears a sob.

"Silly bear, why are you crying?" This is it, the fall from the edge. A knot chokes him; he doesn't want this to end. Yes, it feels like the train's roaring away, tracks fading fast, *but it ain't over till it's over.* "I'm not trying to make it hard; I'm trying to make it impossible." She doesn't want this to end either, he hopes. A watery sheen filters his vision. *It's only a hard talk, that's all it is; it's just hard.* Love gets through tough talks. Arguments happen. "Look, don't do this. It obviously upsets you, and that should tell you it's not right to do this." There is a word, a phrase, something that's going to crystallize everything, to lock it all back into place.

"Baby, please! Silly bear." *Was that a goodbye?* "No, don't you say that, not yet." He breathes, sharp and shallow. "Bella, Bella. Listen to me, okay? I'm sorry. Alright? I'm sorry if I was never able to give you what you needed. I'm sorry if I didn't leave you enough little notes in the morning before I used to go to class. I'm sorry that I played video games too much or didn't notice your makeup. I don't want to lose you, and I'm sorry if I am because I wasn't what you needed me to be."

That's it. He's not there. He needs to be there. Home is a dream he had long ago; it fades with the dawn. *His home is with her.* "Would it make a difference if I told you I was willing to give up all that I thought made me who I am to set up my life out there with you? If that's what it takes, I will." His voice scrapes, raw and frayed; every word is the truth, every damn one. No matter, it's not getting through. He doesn't understand why she can't hear the vow in it, the purity, the honesty.

"Please, then tell me, is there somebody else?" Wet eyes on a drowning man, grasping anything in desperation, even the weight that drags him down faster. "Then why? Why?" The beige world turns to black.

"Wait, wait, I go first. I love you, Bella. My Silly Bear. Goodbye."

Click.

"I thought I had somebody down for me

It turns out

You were making a fool of me, ohhh

It's not right, But it's okay"

-Whitney Houston

ELEVEN

IT'S NOT RIGHT, BUT IT'S OKAY

The scorching sun beats down on the bleached concrete, its heat shimmering in waves. Jared sits on the stoop of his house, crumpling the greasy yellow wrapper of his devoured cheeseburger. Lucas indulges in the final morsel of his own.

"You want to go to the city tonight?" Jared shoots the wrapper at the garbage can but misses, watching it land in the grass.

"I think there's something going on at Quest tonight," Lucas responds, tossing his wrapper into the garbage with a casual flick.

Jared shakes his head and grimaces. "Oh, we could do that. Who's going?"

"I don't know, probably you, me, and Donnie." Lucas squints up at the glaring sky, his face scrunching against the brightness. "I think Frisco might actually come out."

"No, what happened? Did the lanes burn down or something?" Jared responds with sarcastic concern.

Lucas turns to Jared, and in sync, they raise their eyebrows and arms, punctuating the idea with a solid, *"Could be."* The boys share a light laugh, then sit silently as the chirping birds dart through the blue sky above.

Jared's fingers drum on his knees, the sudden quiet pressing in. He grabs a French fry from the container, chomps on it, and looks down at his front jeans pocket. He reaches in and pulls out a folded piece of paper. Jared peers over at Lucas, whose focus has shifted from the blue sky to the denim-blue backside of a pair of girls walking away at the end of the block. Jared extends his arm and taps the paper into Lucas's chest.

"What's this?" Lucas grabs the paper from Jared's hand and begins to unfold it.

"Just a bunch of stuff that's been bothering me," Jared says, looking down at the pebbled and cracked stoop, dodging Lucas's gaze.

Lucas stops fiddling with the note and stares at Jared. "You've got to be kidding me."

Jared quickly turns to Lucas, putting his hands up in explanation. "Nothing bad."

"What's it say?"

"I think you're missing the point of what a letter is," Jared can't help grinning, savoring his quick wit. "You see, you have this piece of paper with words, and then you read those words."

"Alright, ass." Lucas slips the note into his pocket.

"Well, aren't you gonna read it?" Jared's smile shifts to a baffled, open-mouthed stare.

"I think you're missing the point of what a letter is," Lucas loves nothing more than tossing a joke back at a jokester. "You see, you are given a piece of paper with words, and then you read those words whenever you want to."

Jared snags another salty fry. "Fair enough. But do me a favor when you do read it; tell me what you think." Jared bites down.

Angie blows away the steam curling from her mug and sips her tea, two sugars melting into a milky swirl. She sits across the kitchen table, watching Joseph swirl soggy cereal drowned in milk. She's been observing him since she came down to put the kettle on. Back then, the cereal was fresh, but now it sits untouched as the kettle's whistle fades and her cup fills.

"Do you want to talk about it?" Angie thinks there's only so long Joseph can find peace hypnotizing himself in his cereal's multi-colored, faux fruit-flavored whirlpool.

"No, I don't want to talk about it." It's not much of an answer, but it's better than silence. Angie sips her tea, poised for the quiet to crack. She needs to stay patient, to hover close and wait.

Joseph, done with his uneaten breakfast, carries the bowl to the sink and sets it down. He shuffles back to the table and sits, his eyes lingering on the location where the bowl had been. Angie follows his movements, drains the bowl into the sink, dispatches the cereal into the trash, and rinses it with a trickle of cold water.

"I'm sorry. I didn't mean to snap at you." Joseph's voice is quiet, his head drooping, a weight pulling his chin down, his eyes fixed on the empty table. "I don't know what to do. What should I have said? What should I do?"

Angie tears off a paper towel and wipes the damp bowl. "It's not your fault, Joseph. Sometimes, things simply aren't meant to be." She sets the bowl aside to dry and returns to her tea at the table. "She was never going to leave Michigan, and deep down, a part of you knew that."

In the quiet of the kitchen, in the space between mother and son, there's nowhere for Joseph to hide from the truth. "I tried everything I could think of. And I meant it all. I love her." He hesitates, the next words sticky on his tongue. If he must face the truth, so should his mother. *"I never should've left."*

"Joseph, I know right now it seems bad, but it'll get better. It's for the best." His eyes lift from the tabletop, searching for comfort she won't give. Angie's gaze hardens; no sugarcoating today. The best medicine for heartache is the truth, raw and unsparing. She'll wrench it off, like an old bandage, and make him face it. "You wouldn't have truly been happy out there. Instead of two years, who knows, maybe it would've taken ten until things fell apart. And then you'd be missing ten years."

Joseph closes his eyes, tears slipping down. His fingers pinch the bridge of his nose, and he spreads them back and forth, smearing droplets across his eyelids. "But how do you know things will get better? You and Daddy always had each other since you were like twelve?" Wet streaks stain his cheeks, unstoppable. "What if it doesn't? What if, at least once every day, she'll pop into my head?"

Angie sips her tea. So often with her children, answers leap to her lips before their words fully form. Their lives, with all their moving parts, leave little room for pause, always another task waiting. But this morning, her patience settles, steady and calm. Her fingers twitch, itching to coddle him with easy lies. Each sip fights against a maddening urge to get on with the day, to clean up the emotional spill in a tidy fashion. That would be a mistake, a lesson she learned with Lucas. She didn't take enough time then, and look at him now. Assuming he was too young for such intense emotions, she figured they'd fade fast, and she was wrong. She refuses to fail Joseph the same way. He's supposed to be a man, his teenage years behind him, and when talking to a man, you talk to him straight.

"I'm not going to lie; she probably will." Angie sets her mug down, and a small wet ring dampens the table as a slight drip escapes the lip, gliding down onto her fingers. Her eyes never move; she holds her son's gaze, offering no escape. "But you'll love someone else." A short burst of air escapes Joseph's lips. She raises a finger, cutting off any retort. "It won't be the same, but it will be just as good and just as right."

Angie pauses, her eyes tracing his face for a flicker of understanding. Joseph glances toward the entryway as Lucas hurries into the kitchen and grabs a bowl. He fills it with cereal and sits between them, gleefully snatching the gallon of milk and pouring. A splash of milk spills onto the table, but Lucas ignores the mess and digs into the sugary mixture.

The kitchen falls still, hushed except for Lucas's crunching. The grinding of his teeth rings in his ears, a shiver prickling his neck. "What's the matter?"

Joseph slaps the table near the spill. "Nothing." He throws a napkin at Lucas and storms out. Lucas calls after him, a bright pink pebble slipping from his mouth, skidding past his chin to the floor. "What happened?"

"Bella broke up with him," Angie says, rising to carry her cup to the sink.

"Oh," Lucas swallows, eyeing the empty seat. He picks up the napkin and wipes at the spilled milk.

Frisco, lucky enough to snag a decent parking spot, turns the wheel slowly and backs his car into the tight space. Most of the time, they'd be stuck parking a block or two away, so despite the cramped fit, he takes his time and nestles the car between a dark blue BMW and a sporty but banged-up Nissan Maxima. Frisco cracks open his door cautiously, avoiding contact with the neighboring car. He sucks in his gut and shuffles out. Donnie, with no such qualms, swings the rear door open with a bang. A small white mark appears where his door grazes the Nissan. Donnie lifts a shoulder at Frisco's accusing glance, licks his finger, rubs the spot, and moves on. Jared eyes the gap, then slips out carefully behind him, leaving the Nissan untouched.

Lucas lingers in the shotgun seat, his face unmoved by their arrival, the distant hum of traffic drifting through the air. His eyes are glossy and dull, lids half-lowered, burdened with thought. Streetlights scatter their glow against the windshield. His head rests against the passenger-side window, a perfect target for Donnie's attention-grabbing fist.

"Lou, we're here," Donnie slams his hand on the glass, sending a shockwave that jolts Lucas from his daze.

Shaking off the fog, Lucas exits the car and joins his friends in the lot. Donnie bounds ahead, his movements almost a skip, weaving through the parking lot toward the line of bodies awaiting entry into the Quest nightclub. "Come on. Let's go!"

"Oh, what's your rush? You just can't wait to hang out on the wall and not talk to any girls while I'm hooking up?" The night air and the crowd's murmur coax a sly smile onto Lucas's face as he saddles up to his eager friends.

"Hmm yes, suck my balls." Donnie salutes Lucas with twin middle fingers and spins toward the club's entrance. The air carries the tang of pre-game beers and perfume. Bass from inside pulses through the pavement, syncing with the crowd's restless shuffle. The line snakes along the brick wall, a mix of smoking twenty-somethings in tight outfits and almost-twenty-somethings in skimpier ones, their curves backlit by the neon glow of the sign above.

Lucas, still clearing his haze, trails behind. Jared saddles up alongside him, "What's the matter? You seem a little off?"

Lucas doesn't answer right away. He adjusts his shirt collar, eyes tracing the gleam of headlights on a row of nearby cars. "Nothing. Just the house; it's too crowded."

His strides slow; Frisco and Donnie pull farther ahead. "I can't get any sleep. My back hurts from being on the basement couch. Never mind, it's always freezing down there."

Jared, noting the gap, stops walking. "So, did you read the letter?"

Lucas nods, his eyes still on the cars.

"What'd you think?"

"I don't know."

Lucas blinks, slow and deliberate, then meets Jared's eyes. Jared nods once, accepting the vague reply, and turns toward the club. "What were your brothers doing tonight?"

"I think Tony was at Jackie's. I don't know what Joe's doing." Lucas glances at the line trailing from the entrance. "I asked him to come, but he didn't want to."

Jared raises an eyebrow, *Lucas asking his brother to come? That's new.* He follows Lucas's drifting gaze, which darts around the lot and lands in a dark corner. Under a flickering streetlight, he spots the hood of a familiar car. "Hey, isn't that your ex's car?" The question snaps Lucas's focus, igniting a quickness in his step toward the entrance.

Donnie waves them forward, wedging into a gap near the front of the line.

"Let's go."

Men in sleek, button-down shirts, unbuttoned to flaunt shaved chests, sport shiny diamond-encrusted crosses that swing to and fro on gold chains. Women in shoulder-baring tops shimmer above sequined belts, their jeans clinging like a second skin. Each body glows in the pulsing lights of the DJ. Packed tight, the dancers make the floor flex in time with their moves. A blast of compressed air shoots over the cheering crowd, and billows of smoke swirl through the air, sparkling like clouds. Reina's insistence that *No One's Gonna Change You* cuts through the haze, drawing even more bodies onto the dance floor. Hips grind, arms roll, chins lift toward the ceiling; all in praise of Jonathan Peters' remix artistry.

Lucas finds himself at the heart of it, his body weaving through the crowd. He shares smiles with women swaying with abandon as they meet cheek to cheek. He swigs his beer and lets the music wash over him. Spinning into a sliver of space, he unleashes his moves with a wild shimmy, drawing a receptive female partner in return.

In his own pocket of freedom, Jared dances solo, immersed in his choreography, consumed by the beat. Frisco hovers nearby, stiff in his movements, swaying lightly from side to side. He watches a pair of guys engage in a glow stick battle, each fist wrapped in neon, trails of light streaking the air with each dance move. Donnie, a few feet off the dance floor, leans against a wall, sipping his drink and enjoying the show as two midriff-baring women dance close together.

As the music shifts, it pulls Jared from his rhythm, his thirst clawing at him. He mimes holding a glass to Frisco and points at the invisible drink.

"I'm good," Frisco shouts over the noise, raising his real drink toward Jared.

Jared weaves through the throng of people exiting the bustling dance floor, heading for the equally crowded bar. Stressing over the packed counter, he picks up his pace as a spot materializes up ahead. *Perhaps the bartender will get to me right away,* he hopes, leaning over the grimy surface to signal the server. As he waves, he slips on the slick bar and collides with a fellow club-goer to his right, spilling the man's drink. The displaced club-goer turns to face an apologetic Jared. Jared grabs a stack of cocktail napkins and goes to hand them over but stops, recognizing a face half-remembered from high school.

"Hey Sal, how have you been doing?" Jared asks, hoping the recognition will ease the tension.

"I thought it was you." Sal takes the napkins and wipes at the clear liquid dripping down his chest.

"It's been ages, man. Sorry, I'll get you a new one. What are you drinking?" Jared motions for Sal to squeeze back in beside him; the two of them vying for the bartender might double their chances.

Standing shoulder to shoulder, Sal leans in close to Jared's ear. "Vodka on the rocks, splash of water with a lime."

Jared squirms, his skin prickling as Sal's vodka-laced breath tickles his ear. But everyone's squeezed tight at the bar, and the bass thumps so loud it swallows words; *it might be Sal's leaning in to make sure he's heard.*

"Any particular type of vodka?" Jared asks, nestling closer to the bar in a futile effort to create space.

Sal laughs and points at the dusty bottles. "Doesn't matter. I think most of the bottles are for show anyway; they've got the plastic gallon specials to overcharge us with."

Sal's hand lands on Jared's shoulder, his fingers squeezing into the muscle. They share a laugh as the harried bartender approaches.

Lucas, now solo, grooves to Melanie C's *I Turn To You*, her vocals guiding his movements. Frisco nudges Donnie, laughing at Lucas's exaggerated "dancing." Lucas buys a brightly colored test tube from a scantily clad shot-girl weaving through the crowd. He downs it in one gulp, sticks his tongue out in disgust, and resumes his sloppy hunt for a dance partner.

Then, like a thunderbolt, Lucas stops grooving and cuts a path toward the shapely frame of a girl in a sequined top. Pushing through the crowd, he brushes past dancers and wraps his arms around her waist from the back.

"Uh-oh." Frisco jerks, his posture stiffening in alertness.

In the haze of smoke and lights, Lucas sways with an all-too-familiar pair of hips. His body, no longer a mess of awkward jerks, moves in well-rehearsed time with her form. Frisco's eyes widen as he recognizes that body; he knows this girl; after all, he witnessed the moment she broke his best friend's heart.

"What?" Donnie, distracted by scouting ladies from afar, misses the scene.

Frisco points to the dance floor. "Look who Lucas is dancing with."

"Fucking shit, there goes the night." Donnie unleashes a long sigh, shakes his head, and backs away. "I'm going to get another drink."

Frisco maneuvers through the dense crowd, wading toward Lucas and the ex-girlfriend. She turns to face her mystery partner but locks eyes with Frisco instead, stopping him dead. Realizing it's Lucas who grabbed her, she pushes him off, dismissing his advances, and grabs the nearest well-muscled *guido*. Lucas, following suit, finds a new partner of his own. As their eyes hold each other's, their bodies hold onto different people.

Jared's gaze shifts to the end of the bar. Donnie settles in and waves down the bartender. Certain Donnie hasn't noticed him and Sal, Jared averts his eyes and turns away. The bartender collects the empty glasses and money, returning shortly with two chilled cocktails. Sal clinks his glass against Jared's and takes a slow sip from its rim, licking his top lip when finished.

Jared's posture stiffens as Sal's eyes encase him. "Well, it was nice running into you, but, uh, I've got to get going."

Sal grabs Jared's arm, his thumb rubbing up and down. "What's the rush? You on a date?" He nods toward Donnie.

Jared's eyes dart, searching for an escape. "No, I'm with friends."

"Great, maybe I could give you a call sometime? Catch a movie or something, you know, without your friends around." Sal rolls his eyes, tired of the hiding-who-you-are game but familiar with the struggle of keeping up appearances.

"Wait, what?" The alcohol in Jared's system slams to a halt; his brain fires off a warning. "Look, I hate to hurt your feelings, but I'm not interested."

Sal removes his hand, purses his lips, and gazes at his drink.

"Besides, I'm not, you know, *that way.*"

Sal bursts into laughter, spilling a bit of his drink.

"You're not!?" He snickers. "You're kidding, right? I'm sorry, I just thought..." Sal shakes his head, patting Jared's arm. "Well, color me embarrassed. I got to go." He leans in, placing a palm flat on Jared's chest. "Do me a favor, don't mention this to anybody, okay?" His eyes hold a flicker of fear before he turns and walks off.

Jared tracks Sal's retreat until a hand lands on his shoulder from behind, making him flinch.

"Didn't we use to go to high school with that kid?" Donnie slides into Sal's spot.

Jared slaps Donnie's chest. "Yeah, now you wanna talk about being gay, that kid's gay."

Donnie's eyes bulge, his mouth agape with glee. "How do you know?"

"Because he just hit on me." Jared punctuates each word with a slap to Donnie's shoulder.

The last time Donnie was this excited was when Bill Clinton was caught getting head in the White House. "No way that kid turned fag. Holy shit!" He leans closer, breath reeking of cheap beer. "Wait, what? He hit on you? Like, full-on?" Donnie throws his head back and cackles, loud enough to turn heads. "Oh, man, that's gold!"

"What, no quip about me?" Jared sets his drink down and crosses his arms.

"Dude, I know you're not seriously dipping your wand in the chocolate fun dip. I just like to fuck with you, but that kid's a true-to-life homosexual." Donnie pops onto his tiptoes, craning his neck to spot Sal disappearing into the flashing lights. "I gotta see this kid again. Maybe he'll ask me out!"

"I don't see what's the big deal. Let him do what he wants to do." Jared relaxes, then frowns. Donnie's reaction feels off. It's nearly the new millennium after all, and it's not like being gay is a shocking human discovery. Movies like *Philadelphia* and *In & Out* were box-office hits, George Michael got outed at a rest stop, and no one batted an eye. "You seriously don't think I'm gay?"

Donnie laughs. "No asshole, but then again with that shirt..." He shrugs. "Did he try to kiss you or what?"

Jared gives him one last shove, and they walk off with fresh drinks.

Frisco catches up and nods toward Lucas.

Lucas's dancing devolves into a stumbling mess. Dancers around him smirk and share judgmental glances.

"We have to leave," Frisco says.

Donnie scoffs, shoving his drink toward Frisco. "I just got a drink, it took like a year!"

Frisco grabs Donnie's face and forces him to look at Lucas. Lucas staggers, his body lurching out of sync with the bass. He raises his rose-colored drink, but it slips, shattering on the floor in a spray of ice and glass. Frisco rushes to his side, voice soft but urgent. "Come on, Lou, we have to go."

Lucas's glassy eyes shift from the mess to his ex, wrapped around another guy, her gaze locked elsewhere. He turns to Frisco, his smile hollow and slurred. "No way! Where's my drink?"

Jared and Donnie catch up as Frisco tightens his grip on Lucas's arm, tugging him toward the exit. "Come on, everyone's getting bored. It's time to go."

"Yeah, Lou, this place is dead. Let's call it a night." Donnie chimes in, catching Frisco's eye. Frisco mouths a silent thanks.

Lucas's eyes widen, his mouth hanging open in a drunken stupor. He stamps his feet and flails his arms like a toddler mid-meltdown.

"Well, I'm leaving," Frisco says, jingling his keys. "And since none of you brought your cars, I suggest you come with me."

Lucas waves him off and resumes his sloppy dance. Frisco signals to the others that he's going. Jared wobbles between Lucas and his ex, mirroring Lucas's every move to block his view. "Come on," Jared urges.

Lucas relents, letting Jared lead him through the crowd and into the humid summer night. The thumping music muffles as they stagger outside. In the sticky air, Lucas takes in each friend and mutters, "You guys suck."

Passing a few casual smokers, Frisco presses the unlock button on his key fob. His car blares its horn and flashes its lights, alerting the boys. Lucas, trailing behind, lingers near the nightclub's exit, his eyes fixed on the crowd spilling out.

Frisco reaches the car and exhales in relief, thankful the worst was a broken glass, not a full-out brawl. Jared opens the door and hops inside, waiting for Lucas. But Lucas doesn't follow. Jared scans the lot and spots him staring at his ex-girlfriend, her arm linked with the guy she was dancing with, laughing as they head toward the parking lot.

Lucas's fists clench, his jaw tight. He storms toward the couple, his footfalls landing with purpose. Frisco, catching the movement, shouts, "Lucas, take it easy!"

Unfazed, Lucas closes the distance, his voice low and sharp. "Hey, you. Yeah, you with her." The guy, tall and broad, turns, smirking as he sizes Lucas up. Lucas's eyes burn, locked on the stranger. "You think you can just..."

Jared's eyes widen as Lucas shoves the guy, sparking a shout from the ex-girlfriend. Jared sprints across the lot, shouting, "Lucas, cut the shit!" A flash of red and blue sparks his eye; a cop car cruises slowly along the street bordering the lot, its lights slicing through the dark.

Lucas's nostrils flare, spit spraying as he snarls, "Fuck this guy." The stranger shoves back, words lost in the rising chaos. "Fuck her."

Frisco stands at the open door of his vehicle, nervously scanning the lot. Smokers and bystanders point toward Lucas, and Frisco yells in a panic, "We gotta go, guys!"

Jared reaches Lucas, grabbing his arm to pull him back as the stranger swings a wild punch, grazing Lucas's shoulder. The cop car slows, its headlights sweeping closer. Jared ducks, yelling at Frisco, "I got this. Chill!"

Lucas throws down, landing a hard jab to the guy's chest, stumbling him backward into a parked car, setting off its alarm.

"Stop!" Jared hollers, his jaw clenched, voice sharp and splintering, eyes darting to the approaching police lights.

Lucas seethes, shaking, chest heaving. "Why does she get to do this?" He gets in Jared's face. "Fucking asshole." He paces, kicking at the gravel. "Not like it's her, fuck his shit."

Jared snaps, grabbing Lucas's shoulders, his voice urgent as the cop car's engine hums closer. "You're right! Fuck her, fuck this guy, but you know what? Fuck you. I don't feel like getting arrested tonight, asshole!"

Surprisingly, Jared's words pierce Lucas's rage. Glancing at the cop car now idling at the lot's edge, Lucas sprints toward Frisco's car as its engine roars to life. Jared and Lucas hop inside, slam the doors, and the screech of Frisco's tires mixes with the blaring of alarms, drowning out the music from the club as they speed away from the flashing lights.

"Sometimes I want to cry
And sometimes I want to die
Please help me understand
Why can't my heart just lie?"
-Deborah Cox

TWELVE

THINGS JUST AIN'T THE SAME

Labor Day isn't until the sixth, and the autumnal equinox is scheduled to land on the twenty-third of September, but for Sinclair Avenue this Saturday, August twenty-first, nineteen ninety-nine, it's the last day of summer. The last car rolls away as neighbors clear the street for their yearly block party. They prepare tables under a cloudless summer sky, coolers brimming with ice-cold sodas and beers lined up beside each one. Children chase each other across the empty blacktop, their sneakers squeaking as they revel in the traffic-free street.

Music from the DJ, stationed in the avenue's center, fills the air. Laughter and joyful screams echo as children see-saw on the yellow-and-blue sky swing truck, their shrieks mingling with the gossip of their parents. Colorful inflatable bounce houses send them tumbling; some land on their feet, most on their backsides. Guests from nearby houses trickle in, swelling the crowd as the day wears on.

The early afternoon sun beats down, hot but not unbearable for late August, a perfect day to hang outside with the boys.

Lucas scowls as he cracks open a fresh beer. Tomorrow the Vitagliano family would start preparing for the long drive to Columbus, Ohio, and his lips curl at the thought of yet another trip to the Midwest – this time for his sister's graduation.

Jared and Hatcher sit close, munching on chips as Frisco exits the house, arms full of folding chairs, and places them around the table. Donnie, the only local, leaves his family's table and saunters over.

"So, what do you want to do?" Donnie asks, fishing a beer from the battered red cooler by Lucas's side.

He cracks it open with a sharp hiss.

Lucas takes a long swig of his beer and shrugs.

"Let's shoot some hoops," Hatcher blurts, spraying bits of half-eaten chips onto the table.

Nodding in sync, Frisco and Hatcher rise from their chairs. They make their way toward the driveway basketball hoop, where a few younger kids bounce a ball in a lazy game of pass-around. Hatcher barges in, snagging a rebound and hoisting the ball high. He laughs as the kids leap around him, their small hands clawing at the air to snatch it back.

Lucas sets his beer down with a soft clink and stands. Jared follows, tilting his head toward the others. "Hey, Lou, about that letter—did you talk to them yet?"

Lucas shakes his head, a chuckle rumbling out. "Yeah, we pretty much all agreed to stop calling you names and making fun of you like that."

"Thanks," Jared says, a touch of relief in his voice.

"We also agreed that it was a pretty gay way of going about it," Lucas adds, smirking.

Jared rolls his eyes and grins. "Har har, very funny."

Lucas's smirk fades, his voice dropping as he meets Jared's gaze. "Seriously though, don't hold shit back. If something's bothering you, just say it, man. We're your friends."

Hatcher lobs the basketball to Lucas. Before the kids can swarm him, he bounces it to Frisco with a flick of his wrist. The children, sensing their game's collapse, scatter down the street, already chasing some new adventure.

As Lucas and Jared make their way toward the basketball hoop, Joseph emerges from the house and dumps fresh ice into the cooler.

Hatcher points at Joseph, "Good, there's your brother, even teams." Lucas turns and catches a glimpse of his brother as the clatter from the refreshed ice dies down.

Joseph's not dressed for basketball or for being seen in public, really. His shorts, cut-down sweatpants, frayed and stained at the knees, hang loose around his waist. His guinea tee hasn't seen a wash in weeks; it's yellowed and clinging to his sweat-soaked frame.

Lucas hasn't seen much of his brother over the last week. He's sure Joseph was wearing the same outfit three days ago, but it's hard to tell. Joseph's been holed up in the bedroom, door shut tight. When he does emerge for a quick trip to the bathroom or to grab a small snack, he keeps his Discman clutched in one hand, headphones clamped over his ears, the faint buzz of music leaking out. There's no talking to him.

Even when he ducks into the bathroom, Joseph skips shaving. His usual light scruff has grown into something scraggy and dark. His hair's a mess too, no comb, no attempt at style. It sticks up in tufts, flattened in spots, like the pillow's his only stylist.

"Joe, come here, you're our sixth man," Hatcher says, tossing the ball his way. Joseph catches it on instinct and then lifts his face from the ball to the group, squinting against the glaring sun.

Lucas, half-expecting Joseph to toss the ball aside and retreat to the safety of the house, is surprised when his brother jogs over instead.

"What's the teams?" Joseph asks.

"Me, you, Jared. Versus. Play to fifty," Hatcher blurts, setting the stakes without waiting for input.

"Fifty?" Joseph winces. *There it is,* Lucas thinks, his brother's eyes drop, a telltale sign he's about to bail.

"What's the matter, out of shape?" Frisco teases, stretching his arms around his back.

Joseph fires a hard pass that thumps Frisco in the chest. "A little, but look who's talking."

Frisco launches a shot that clangs off the rim and bounces away. "Yeah, but have you ever scored three goals in one game to lead your team to the playoffs?"

Joseph darts over, snagging the rebound mid-bounce, and starts dribbling in place. The boys spread around the hoop, claiming their positions. Joseph bounce-checks the ball to Frisco, and the game is underway.

A New York pick-up game isn't the polished basketball of TV or proper courts. No one's flopping for fouls or calling charges; if you're not pushing, you're not playing. Joseph isn't a natural, missing more shots than he makes, but he refuses to yield an inch. He leans into the contact, grinning as he jostles for position, embracing the street game's rough edges.

Sweat trickles down temples and gathers on brows as the game heats up. Lucas and Hatcher never miss a layup, quick under the net to snatch rebounds for both sides. Donnie and Jared hold their own, sinking the occasional shot but bricking others. Frisco, despite his bravado, often passes the ball when the lane opens up, shying away from the shot.

As the game drags on, Joseph's breath rasps in short, jagged bursts. His legs, heavy as lead, lag behind his will, and his arms flail, too sloppy to sink the ball or shield it from swats. Each bump from another player crashes harder against the tightness in his chest. A cramp claws at his side, twisting his torso with sharp, relentless stabs of pain. He's stuck on defense, narrowly holding his ground.

Lucas charges in. Joseph lunges for the ball but smacks his brother's elbow instead. Jared snags the loose ball, flings it to Frisco, who fires it back to Lucas. Lucas springs for a layup, but Joseph stumbles into him midair, sending him skidding across the pavement.

Lucas slams his palm down and scrambles up. "God! You can't do that! Every time I go up for a shot or a goddamn rebound..."

"What the hell are you talking about?" Joseph snaps, cutting him off. "I look around, and I see you touching this one, jumping on that one!"

"No. I jump straight up. You jump, and your ass lands on my shoulder. Besides, you push!"

"I've been getting pushed the whole game!" Joseph grabs fistfuls of his hair, yanking hard as his face flushes red and quivers with fury.

Lucas snags the ball off the ground and rams it into his brother's chest.

"That's because you don't know what you're doing!" he shouts.

Joseph snatches the ball, knuckles white with rage, and tears it from Lucas. "Fine, fuck you! I'm sick of this shit, all you do is bitch." Stares from a neighbor's crowd lock onto them, the argument too loud to ignore.

Lucas spins away, shouting at his teammates, "I'm getting killed out here."

But Joseph isn't done. The game's rough play has cracked the numbness he's felt since the breakup, each shove and shout stoking a fire he didn't know was still burning. He's not enjoying the game; he's feeding on the fury it's unleashed. With a guttural yell, he punts the basketball, and it bounces into the middle of the street as the onlookers scatter. Then he turns and stalks off.

"Come on. Stop. Let's finish the game. What's the big deal?" Frisco's voice slices through the block party's roar, freezing Joseph near the folding table.

"The big deal is he's being an asshole, and I don't want to play anymore!" Joseph swipes a beer from the table and hurls it toward the hoop. The bottle spins across the concrete, foam spraying as it shatters.

Donnie sprints down the street, snatching the ball from some kid who scooped it up. Lucas claps a hand on Frisco's shoulder. "Forget it, let him go. Was I wrong?"

"No, you were right." Frisco shakes his head. "I don't know why he got so upset."

Joseph charges back, his steps thudding like a runaway engine. "What?! What the fuck did you just say?"

Frisco throws up his hands, palms out, as if to fend off Joseph's advance.

"Nothing, just…"

Jared wedges himself between them, catching a spray of spit as Joseph leans in, his face inches from Frisco's. "Just what? If you have something to say to me, you say it to me! You thought I was wrong, fucking say it! Otherwise, don't ever get in the middle of my brother and me again. He's my fucking brother, not yours. This is *my* family!"

Joseph glimpses a small child behind Frisco, her eyes full of fear. His anger sours into shame, his neck tingling under the crowd's silent stares. Without a word, he turns and storms back into the house.

Donnie jogs back, ball in hand, and sinks a clean shot through the net. "Nothing but net!" He scoops up his own rebound, then freezes, scanning the guys' tense faces. "What?"

"Con te partirò
Paesi che non ho mai
Veduto e vissuto con te
Adesso si li vivrò
Con te partirò"
-Andrea Boccelli

Thirteen

CON TE PARTIRÒ

The front door slams, yanking Angie's attention. She rises from her seat at the kitchen table, assuming her son is rushing in for a drink or to refill the cooler outside. Instead, she watches him pace behind the door, mumbling to himself.

"Joseph, you got something in the mail today," Angie calls out, halting his restless pacing. Joseph turns toward her, but his gaze slides past, as if she's part of the furniture. Angie stands, grabs a compact kraft-paper package off the table, and holds it out.

"What is it?" Joseph asks, his eyes shifting from blankness to the box.

"I don't know," Angie says, setting the package back on the table. "Open it and find out."

Joseph strides into the kitchen, his eyes locked on the package. He snatches it, tears open the small brown box, and reveals a black velvet jewelry case inside. He snaps open the clamshell and stares down at a refurbished Michigan State University ring, its gleam catching the light. It appears like new, as if it were minted yesterday, every detail sharp and eye-catching. The bold, raised numbers of the graduating year, 1999, adorn the right side, while the left features the letters *B.S.* as a scroll engraved with "Chemistry" curls around a beaker.

Joseph's eyes linger on the ring's emerald, where a gold-plated Spartan helmet glints in the center. His fingers hover over the stone, tracing the helmet without touching it. The emerald's glow dims as he shuts the lid with a soft click. He slips the box into his pocket and heads upstairs. His mother stays in the kitchen, her brow furrowing as he climbs upward in silence.

Joseph enters his room, a storm of conflicting emotions: numbness, anger, and disgust churning in his gut. His mind swirls with recent memories: his brother's face, the reek of Frisco's breath, the hollow echo of a goodbye through a telephone headset. The tightness in his chest surges into unease, and he snatches an orange stuffed lion from Anthony's bed, hurling it across the room without a thought.

The lion sails through the air, clips the bureau with a dull thud, and sends cologne bottles tumbling. It ricochets off the mirrored closet door and falls crumpled to the floor, photos following, fluttering down like autumn leaves caught in a sudden gust.

The lion lies limp and deflated, a shadow of its former self. Once plump with stuffing, it now sags, a relic of happier times. The photos, dislodged from the brass border of the mirrored doors, await rescue.

Joseph kneels and lifts the lion, recalling how it once brought joy to his brother. He sets it among the pillows and stoops to gather the scattered memories. Each image captures a slice of the past: a boy in a high school cap and gown, a black-haired Anthony in a white suit clutching rosary beads, Lucas mid-leap, muscles taut as he reaches for a soccer ball frozen in flight. He tucks them back into the mirror's frame, then gathers the remaining photos from the floor.

Joseph flips over a face-down photo and stares into his own smiling eyes, his cheeks flushing at the sight. In the image, his arm is slung over Bella's shoulder, a snapshot of hope. Her gaze lovingly turns up toward a Joseph who no longer stands beside her. His hand trembles as he hesitantly turns over the last photo on the ground.

The glossy Polaroid, with its distinctive white border and bulky bottom, reveals its age. Joseph flips it and holds it up to the mirror, carefully sliding it back into place. He focuses on the desaturated face of his grandfather.

Months ago, standing in his grandfather's shoes felt distant. Joseph, who had invoked his grandfather's spirit before hundreds, promising to strive for his family every day, now feels like a failure and a fraud. He doubts there's anything he could do to disappoint his grandfather, yet he's certain he's not living up to that promise.

Joseph's gaze shifts from his grandfather's image to his own reflection. Stubble has thickened into a scruffy beard, and his thinning hair clings to his forehead in greasy strands. Dark circles hollow his eyes, and his nose gleams with oil. *This isn't how Joseph sees himself,* yet here he is, facing this distorted reflection. He knows he's let the days slip away. He can rage at Frisco for meddling, wallow in the pain of parting from Bella, or grieve for a grandfather who lived a full life, but none of them can stare back at him through a mirror.

A new urgency courses through him, clearing the chaos of emotions as he studies his reflection. He hesitates, then leaves the bedroom, tucking the photo of himself and Bella into a drawer, while his grandfather's smile holds steady from its perch on the mirror.

Angie hears Joseph's footsteps descending the staircase. Her face brightens at the sight of her son, and she can't help but smile. "You shaved. You look so much neater."

Joseph laughs at his mother's delight. "It was that bad, huh?" he replies, a grin matching hers.

In the time it took for Joseph to shave and tame his hair, the block party outside has grown, filled with both familiar and unfamiliar faces. Neighbors he hasn't seen all summer mingle with old friends, each with their own stories to share, and the air hums with the promise of a fresh start.

Angie's gaze drops to Joseph's hand. "Did you try it on?"

Joseph, caught up in the moment, had forgotten about the jewelry box. At her reminder, he pulls it from his pocket.

Carefully, he lifts the ring from its velvet bed, unsure if it will fit, and slides it onto his right ring finger. The ring glides on with a cool, unfamiliar weight, grounding him in the moment. It feels strange among his bare fingers, but there's a quiet comfort in its presence.

"It fits," Joseph says.

"I believe in love
To be the center of all things
And I believe in love to be the way"
-Paula Cole

FOURTEEN

I BELIEVE IN LOVE

The Sinclair Avenue block party swells as the day wears on, drawing in more neighborhood teens. The sun dips lower, stretching shadows across the pavement. Lucas, Frisco, and Michael lounge at a table littered with empty beer bottles. Nearby, Donnie, Jared, and Hatcher dive into a pickup game of hoops, their trash talk and fadeaway jumpers blending with the music and laughter shared amongst the party people.

Joseph reaches into the cooler, pulls a beer from the icy slush, and settles into a chair beside Michael. "Hey, Michael, didn't see you. When did you get here?"

"Just a minute ago," Michael replies as Joseph takes a sip from the cold bottle.

Across the table, Lucas scans his older brother's face, a bemused smile curving his lips. "Hey, you shaved. You look so much...*neater.*" His voice lifts on the compliment, eyebrows arching in playful exaggeration.

Joseph's mouth quirks, a dimple creasing his right cheek. "Yeah, I couldn't recognize myself anymore." He takes another sip, his ring clinking against the amber glass. The band weighs on his finger, solid, accomplished, but odd. He pauses, turning his hand to inspect the gold for imperfections. Finding none, he relaxes and glances toward the cooler, where two unfamiliar faces rummage through the ice. One grabs a drink, the other follows, and they head toward the house.

"Who are they?" Joseph asks, nodding toward the strangers.

"They need to use the bathroom," Lucas replies.

Joseph watches the screen door swing shut behind them, then presses further, "So, you know those kids?"

"Yeah, sure," Lucas says, a little too casually.

Frisco eyes Joseph, his gaze flickering between him and the house. He fidgets in his folding chair, a hand muting a sigh. "Hey Joe, can I talk to you?"

Joseph pulls his gaze from the doorway and notices the tension in Frisco's face. The usual easy grin is gone, replaced by something heavier. Without hesitation, Joseph stands, resting a hand on Frisco's shoulder. "Sure, let's take a walk."

As they walk off, Michael shoots Lucas a questioning glance. Lucas rolls his eyes, takes a long swig from his bottle, and waves him off.

All along the block, the bounce houses and swing rides are stowed, yielding to bicycles and spiraling footballs cutting through the cool air. The blacktop, still radiating the day's trapped heat, sends up shimmering waves that distort the streetlights. The scent of grilled food mingles with the earthy smell of trampled grass, while adults, loosened by hours of drinking, laugh louder and dance sloppier with each song. The block party spills beyond the neighborhood, drawing in strangers from nearby streets.

Joseph takes it all in, his eyes scanning the crowd for a familiar face, someone, anyone to break the awkward silence settling between him and Frisco. They near the end of the block, where a parked car barricade lets only those on foot pass. Joseph recognizes the Maritino's house on the corner; his brother's oldest friend lives there, conspicuously absent all summer. He's wondering where he is when Frisco finally finds the courage to speak.

"Look, Joe, I can understand if you got upset with me."

Joseph knows he's not looking at Frisco. His gaze locks on the asphalt, head down, ears open.

"I didn't mean to get in the middle of you and Louie, you're right."

Joseph snaps his gaze from the road, studying Frisco's face. If there's any insincerity, he'll spot it in his eyes.

"You guys are brothers, and whatever goes on between you two is between you two."

His usual bravado vanishes, his bluster and charm peeled away. Joseph glances at his own hands, fists clenched, and wills them to unclench as Frisco continues.

"You know I love this family. I'd do anything for you guys."

For you guys. The words hit like a punch. He means it, not only for Louie but for him, too. Joseph studies him, really seeing him, perhaps for the first time. No performance, no crowd to entertain. Just a man searching for a place to belong and a place where he's welcome.

Joseph exhales, his shoulders easing. "It's not even like that, Giuseppe. I overreacted."

Frisco's chest lifts with a breath he'd been holding.

"I lost my temper, alright, I'm sorry. I went inside, cooled off a little."

Joseph opens his arms, and Frisco rushes in fast, wrapping him in a tight hug with two closed-fist pats on the back. The tension dissolves.

As they pull apart, Frisco's grin creeps back, his voice taking on that familiar teasing lilt. "Hey, you shaved. You know, I never noticed it before, but you are one stunningly handsome man."

Joseph smirks. "Yes, I know, it's a curse."

Frisco heads back toward the Vitagliano house, but Joseph lingers. His thoughts drift to Louie's old friend, a quiet unease stirring as he wonders why he hasn't seen him around.

The Maritinos moved onto Sinclair Avenue the week after the Vitaglianos. Back then, the block was a patchwork of half-built homes and empty lots. One summer afternoon, much like this one, a young mother had gone knocking on doors, determined to pry her son away from the Nintendo and into the sunshine.

Nicole Maritino was relentless in her mission to find friends for her son, Vic. Lucky for her, she didn't only find a playmate; she found a family. Vic was the same age as Louie, and he quickly became a fixture in their lives. Angie Vitagliano and Nicole Maritino struck up an easy friendship, their alliance sealed over countless cups of tea and shared laughter, all in the name of keeping the kids outside.

That day sparked a summer tradition of joyful afternoons splashing in the pool, late-night card games, and the occasional basement hang to sneak in a marathon video game session or two – despite their mothers' wishes.

Years later, Joseph finds himself standing on the Maritinos' doorstep, the memories of those summer days still fresh in his mind. He knocks, and almost immediately, the door swings open.

"Joseph!" Nicole's voice rings out, warm and welcoming as ever. She ushers him inside before he can say a word, and in the blink of an eye, there's a glass of water in his hand, followed by a deluge of rapid-fire questions, too fast to answer.

"Vic! Come down!" she calls.

The thunder of hurried footsteps follows, and Vic Maritino shoots down. Vic was stocky as a kid, but high school football slimmed him down. Now, a couple of years later, the weight is creeping back, settling on him like it fits.

"Oh, Joseph, I was just getting ready to come down and see you guys," Vic grins.

Joseph can't help but smile. He's always liked Vic. Though Vic's bond with Lucas is tighter, they've forged their own friendship, too.

"Where you been? I haven't seen you all summer," Joseph says.

Vic plants a quick kiss on his mom's cheek, claps Joseph on the shoulder, and moves toward the door. "Yeah, I know. I've been taking summer courses over at St. John's."

Joseph flashes his ring, tapping it with a grin. "Summer courses are the worst. I'm glad I don't have to deal with that anymore."

They head down the block toward the Vitagliano house, Vic's step light with anticipation after a long summer of grind. At the folding table, warm hugs and hand slaps greet him from the whole crew. Donnie tosses him a beer, and Joseph grabs a fresh one from the cooler.

"So what have you been doing with yourself since you graduated?" Vic asks, twisting off the cap with a flick of his wrist.

"Not much, really," Joseph admits, his voice tinged with uncertainty. "I have a resume ready, but I haven't sent it out anywhere yet. My cousin Reggio works at this lab, so I'm planning to apply there first." He cracks open his beer, the hiss sharp in the air, and takes a sip. "Hopefully they'll take me."

Donnie slams the table, sending a few potato chips skittering to the ground. "What, are you kidding me? You were valedictorian, man. They're going to be on your dick." Before Joseph can respond, Donnie snatches his beer and raises it high. "It's like, 'Hey buddy, can I work here?' and they'll be like, 'Holy shit, yeah!'" He grins, then amps up the joke, thrusting the bottle in and out of his mouth in a crude mimicry. "Come here, let's throw in this blow job as well." He licks the bottle's rim, cupping the bottom with exaggerated care.

"From your mouth to God's ears, the censored version, hopefully," Joseph says as Donnie keeps up the crude act, grinning as Joseph smacks his arm. "I do want the job, for Christ's sake."

Donnie laughs and starts downing the stolen beer. Joseph heads back to the cooler for another. As he reaches in, he notices the crowd has thinned; most of the younger kids are gone.

"What happened to all the kids?" he asks, scanning the dwindling partygoers.

Donnie shrugs.

"Where's Louie?" Vic chimes in.

Donnie nods toward the house. "Inside. Be back out soon, I guess."

The streetlights flicker on overhead, and Michael checks his watch. "Joe, when does the wrestling start?"

"I'm not sure. I think around now. You want to go in and check? I'll meet you in the basement," Joseph replies.

"All right." Michael pushes himself up, wobbling as the alcohol springs up on him. He sways like he's on a ship's deck, then steadies himself and stumbles toward the house.

Joseph surveys the table, noticing the drinks have caught up with more than just Michael. "You guys want to come in and watch?"

Donnie, polishing off his latest beer, lets loose a small burp. "No thanks."

"When you see Louie, let him know I'd like to see him," Vic requests.

Joseph leans back, then edges closer. "When was the last time you guys hung out?"

Vic shrugs. "Just been busy."

Joseph senses there's more to it, but for now he lets it slide. Something else nags at him, something he's been avoiding but can't shake. He hesitates, then asks, "Can I ask you something about my brother? What happened?" He knows Lucas wouldn't like him prying, but maybe he needs to.

Vic shifts his gaze to meet Joseph's, his eyes narrowing slightly. "What, with Jessica?"

Joseph's brow furrows. "Whoever." Another chapter he's missed in Lucas's life, another *what-if* to haunt him. If he'd been here, could he have changed things?

Vic scratches his jaw, his fingers brushing the stubble. "She broke his heart." A flush warms his cheeks, and he glances away.

Joseph nods slowly. "I get that. I'm seeing that now." He feels it too, his own heartache shaping his actions, his inability to let go.

"No." Vic shakes his head, his eyes darkening. "It was bad. Wasn't just..." His voice trails off, and he scans the block, his jaw tightening.

If it was heartbreak, Joseph wasn't there then, but he understands it now. Maybe Anthony won't have to suffer like that, but if things with Jackie ever crumble, Joseph swears he won't miss the signs again.

"Forget it, it just... affected him," Vic mutters, trying to dismiss it. Joseph watches Vic's gaze drift to an empty baby carriage on the neighbor's stoop, his eyes misting in the dim light.

Angie's pocketbook lies open on the kitchen table, its contents strewn about. She sifts through it, her movements sharp and frantic, as the front door swings open.

"Did you take money out of my pocketbook?" she snaps, her voice a jagged edge of frustration.

Joseph freezes, head tilting at his mother's panic-stricken rummaging. "No. Why?"

"I noticed my purse stuffed behind the toilet and my cash missing." She stops, blows out a sharp breath, then throws up her hands. "I asked your brother if he took it. He said he didn't, then he left." She points toward the doorway, making Joseph's head snap in that direction.

A realization hits.

"The kids. Those punk kids around the neighborhood." Joseph steps closer, peering into her pocketbook, his eyes scanning as if he can glare the money back into existence.

"I thought it was weird they weren't hanging around anymore."

Without another word, he spins and bolts for the front door. The screen door screeches as he shoves it open, the frame shuddering as it slams against the house.

The group jumps as Joseph slams his hand on the table, his voice cutting through the chatter.

"Come on, let's go find my brother."

Vic leaps up, his chair scraping back. "What's going on?"

"Somebody stole money from my mother's purse, and now Lucas is missing." Joseph's eyes sweep the block, the party's revelry grating against the knot in his stomach.

His brother's not the only one missing.

"Where are Frisco and Jared?" he demands.

"I think I saw them talking to your brother earlier," Donnie mutters, eyes fixed on his beer, avoiding Joseph's stare.

Joseph pins him with a hard glare. No time for games. "Where did they go?"

"Down the block," Donnie says, jerking his thumb toward the end of the street.

Joseph points directly at Donnie, then Hatcher, then Vic. "Let's go."

No hesitation. No debate.

Joseph pivots, his shoes scraping the pavement as he marches down the block, daring the others to follow. To a man, they fall in line. They pick up the pace, moving as one past the DJ, beyond the laughter and lights, turning the corner at the end of Sinclair and onto the downhill slope of Marcy Avenue.

Two blocks down, past the wooded lot where they once played kickball as children, a swarm of teenage boys, close to fifty strong floods the street. They're close enough to hear the music but far enough to dodge adult eyes. They've carved out a makeshift party, free to drink, smoke, and hide from prying eyes.

Joseph and his crew halt.

"Holy shit," Hatcher breathes, summing up what flashes through each of their minds.

"Madone!" Vic mutters.

Donnie, ever the poet, ties a bow on it. "Well, fuck me sideways."

Joseph rocks onto his toes, scanning the sea of bodies for Lucas.

There, at the center of the chaos.

Lucas stands stiff, his usual swagger betrayed by the tight pull of his mouth. A wave of nostalgia crashes through the worry in Joseph's chest: Lucas at seven, dressed as a pirate, breakdancing badly at their sister's Halloween party, the same sheepish grin caught between pride and embarrassment.

Only this time, it's not make-believe.

Joseph's stomach knots as he clocks Frisco and Jared, their bodies pressed tight in the crush of the crowd, eyes darting like trapped animals.

"Louie," Joseph whispers, his breath catching. *None of this is good.*

Vic grabs his arm, snapping him back. "Joe, you alright?"

"Yeah, yeah." Joseph blinks, forcing focus. The night sharpens around him. The weight of his college ring sinks deeper, spreading through his hand, creeping up his arm as he clenches his fist.

"I got this ring back today," Joseph flexes his fingers before curling them into a tight fist. "And now it's going to get all bloody."

He bites down on his knuckle, a small act of bravado for the boys, a weak attempt to convince himself he's ready. It works fine enough. His legs kick back into motion, and the march down Marcy resumes.

"Lucas, please be alright. Please be alright." He whispers, the prayer lingering in the air. But there's no time to wait for an answer.

Inside the circle, Lucas demands answers, his voice steady, daring anyone to step up. "Look, I just want to know who took the money, that's all."

He points at a tall kid, his gelled hair adding inches to his height.

Big Hair laughs and stomps forward. "Nobody here knows what you're talking about."

He glances around, his confidence swelling as if he commands them all, a legion of gold chains and crosses, guinea tees stretched across cologne-drenched bodies, gelled hair locking their thoughts in place.

"So why don't you just take your friends and forget about it," he says, stepping closer to Lucas.

"I let you hang near my house, play ball, use my bathroom," Lucas raises his voice, looking past Big Hair to the rest. "I just want to know who took it. No problems."

Big Hair moves into his line of sight. "Exactly why I'm telling you to go home, so there are no problems."

Lucas stops scanning the crowd and locks eyes with Big Hair.

"You really think this kid's gonna give himself up?" Big Hair smirks, tough only because he's got numbers.

Lucas brushes past him, zeroing in on another kid. The crowd tightens, moving as one, their collective will closing in.

Lucas puffs out his chest and pushes his way through the mob, jabbing his finger at each one, demanding answers. With each shout, he grows more oblivious to the shifting mass around him. Frisco and Jared move in, forming a protective wall, sensing the tension about to snap.

Behind him, creeping slowly, a troublemaker in a Mets cap closes in.

Before he can strike, Joseph shoves through the crowd, rips the kid's cap off, yanking his head backward. "Who you coming up on?" Joseph barks, hurling the hat into the kid's chest.

The kid catches it, flings it to the ground, and chest-bumps Joseph. "Who the fuck are you, man?"

Joseph shoves him back hard. "Who the fuck am I? Who the fuck are you? You take money from my house?"

"What, motherfucker?" No-Hat lunges.

Lucas whips around, eyes blazing at his brother, and darts between them, hands raised. "Get out of here! I can handle this!"

"Handle what?" Joseph snaps, his voice cracking with betrayal. "Look around you, Lucas."

"Get him the fuck out of here," No-Hat orders.

Joseph stands firm. "Why don't you shut your fucking mouth? Did you take the money?" Vic senses the shift and grabs Joseph's shoulder. Joseph smacks his hand away. "I'm not leaving Lucas here."

No-Hat slaps Lucas's arm down and pounds his chest with both fists. "You're not getting anything, so get the fuck out of here."

The crowd surges, their shouts and jeers feeding the chaos.

"Before I bust you up," No-Hat adds, stepping closer.

Frisco yanks Lucas back as Joseph dodges underneath his brother's reach, stepping nose to nose with No-Hat. "Don't you threaten him, bitch!" Joseph yells into the punk's face.

No-Hat shoves him. "Fuck you!"

Lucas snatches No-Hat's shirt and shoves him back into the crowd. Then it hits; he spins, realizing the space around them has shrunk, bodies closing in.

"Come on, then! What? What?" Lucas flings his arms out as far as they can reach, muscles taut as a wire. He pivots, his voice carving the night. "You don't think I kill motherfuckers? Huh! You don't think I do that shit?"

A heartbeat of silence stretches, grave and tense.

The only sound, two and a half blocks away, is the DJ's bass pulsing, its beat thrumming through the air. Lucas's neck veins throb in time with the remix, Real Life's *Send Me an Angel* charging the moment.

No-Hat wrenches loose and lunges.

Frisco grabs for Lucas, trying to help but pulls him off balance instead.

Lucas stumbles, exposed.

No-Hat cocks his fist, lining up a knockout blow to Lucas's temple.

Joseph surges forward, no good; he's too far.

Then, a roar from the crowd.

Out of nowhere, a blonde blur launches through the air.

The weight crashes onto No-Hat's back, arms locking around his throat.

Joseph's breath hitches. *Anthony.*

His little brother, all wiry limbs and wild energy, clings to No-Hat like a feral animal.

And with that, the fragile tension shatters, fifty voices, fifty bodies, all finding their excuse.

The gates of hell swing open.

A chorus of screams and curses erupts, the mob surging toward the brothers.

Big Hair reappears and cracks Lucas across the face. The blow sends Frisco stumbling, his grip lost, both of them hitting the pavement hard.

Two others pounce, boots slamming into Lucas's ribs.

Vic dives on top of his oldest friend, throwing himself over Lucas as a human shield, absorbing the kicks.

Joseph snaps.

He grabs one of the attackers and spins him around. His fingers tighten into a fist around his recently returned ring, the metal digging into his skin.

"Get off my brother!" Joseph bellows.

His fist rockets forward, ring first, and smashes into the asshole's nose with a sickening crunch.

Blood sprays, splattering as the kid staggers back, hands clawing at his ruined face, crimson leaking between his fingers.

Anthony and Hatcher plant their feet, standing back to back, fists raised. Anyone who closes in gets dropped.

The fight explodes.

But the attacks zero in on Lucas. No matter how hard the boys fight, they can't stop them all.

Frisco and Donnie haul Lucas back, dragging him toward the neighboring street, desperate to yank him from the frenzied mob. The crowd surges and swarms, refusing to let him slip away.

Vic clings to Lucas like armor, absorbing the worst of it. A wild kick slams into Vic's head, another crashes into his ribs, but most blows break through. Fists and boots pound Lucas's arms, torso, legs.

Nearby, an oily-faced punk slips through the chaos and rakes his nails down Hatcher's back, tearing his shirt and carving four bloody gashes.

Hatcher hisses in pain, then retaliates.

He twists, fist cocked, and buries a left hook into the punk's cheekbone with a wet thud.

The kid's head jerks to the side, his body folding to the pavement.

Still, the swarm presses in.

Joseph sweeps his eyes over the chaos. Anthony stands firm, holding his ground. Frisco struggles to prop Lucas up, but Jared's lost somewhere in the fog.

Frisco hoists Lucas to his feet, barely ducking a wild right hook from his friend.

"It's me! It's me!" he yells, his voice raw with panic.

Lucas wrenches himself free, shattering Vic's bear-like grip, and charges headfirst into the throng. He kicks, screams, and lands blows on multiple attackers' shins, jaws, and ribs. But the crowd's sheer numbers swallow him. His foot slips on the slick asphalt, and he crashes to the ground again. The mob descends like vultures, fists and feet raining down on him.

Joseph sees their backs turned, and his rage ignites. He swings, fists crashing into every available skull and spine. The crowd reels from the onslaught, a gap splitting open, a sliver's width enough for Vic to lumber in. He plants his massive frame over Lucas, holding back the tide of bodies.

"Get off my brother!" Joseph roars, the words a guttural war cry. His fist smashes into a snarling face. He swings again. *"Get off my brother!"* Knuckles cracking against bone.

A sudden blow splits the back of Joseph's skull. His head whips forward, crashing against the edge of a curb. His knees buckle, and he slumps onto the asphalt, its jagged bite tearing into his palms.

Blood soaks his jeans, gluing them to the street. The dark stain spreads, seeping down toward his shins, thick against his skin.

Memories flash through his mind, sharp and disjointed: standing on stage under blazing lights, Bella's fleeting smile, her voice cutting cold over the phone, spitting fury in Frisco's face, Anthony soaring into the brawl with a wild grin, Lucas crumpled on the ground, a boot smashing into his cheek.

Joseph claws himself up, a raw roar tearing from his chest. His sneakers scrape the blacktop as he steadies himself, but the world tilts and spins. A purple bruise blooms across his arm, spreading like ink over his battered skin.

The blur sharpens into focus, and Joseph realizes he's lagging. The mob's fury ebbs, their movements sluggish now. A few houses down, he spots his crew through the fray. Lucas and Anthony stand shoulder to shoulder, throwing punches. Lucas reckless, Anthony fierce, but retreating inch by inch as Vic and the others tow them back from the chaos.

Joseph barrels forward, body-checking his way through the attackers until he catches up with his brothers. Hatcher has vanished, probably scrapping with Jared somewhere down the street. But if it's just the Vitagliano boys left to throw hands together, well, then that's just the way it's going to be.

Joseph, Lucas, and Anthony jab and weave, their movements a blur of instinct. Fists and footwork drilled into them by their father. The brawl swirls around them, chaotic and violent, but time slows. The punches grow precise, each strike landing with intent. The fight morphs into something controlled, a ballet of rage.

Through Frisco, Vic, and Donnie's urgent shouts, they disengage and run, home ground in sight.

Sinclair Avenue welcomes them like an old friend. They burst onto the opposite corner, crashing into Vic's yard and disrupting the quiet gathering inside. Vic's father, his uncles, and their next-door neighbor sit, cigars in hand, scotch swirling in their glasses. Vic's family is as old-school as they come: kind Italian faces, bright eyes, strong frames softened by time. The moment their eyes land on the boys, disheveled, bruised, and breathing hard, their smiles tighten, their eyes burn. And they rise as one.

Vic, like a third-base coach signaling home, swings his arm in a wide arc, herding his friends into the backyard. Right as he turns to head inside, a hand grabs the back of his shirt.

Instinct kicks in. Vic whips around, his hand clamping around the stranger's throat.

Jared's eyes bulge under the strain. "Vic! It's Jared. Jared."

Joseph jumps in, his hand closing gently around Vic's arm. "Relax. Relax."

Vic's grip slackens. The purple drains from Jared's face, leaving it blotchy and pale and no one mentions it as Hatcher barrels through the crowd. A blow lands from behind. Hatcher spins, unleashing a roundhouse punch, then breaks loose, sprinting into the yard and slamming the gate shut.

The Maritino men station themselves at the entrance, arms crossed, their steely gazes dispersing the punks with a single glance.

As the havoc settles, Vic's father rounds up the boys.

"Is everyone here? Everyone alright? What the hell happened?"

Sweat-soaked and bruised, clothes torn, they huddle under the Maritino roof.

Joseph stares at his hand, knuckles pulsing with pain. His ring lies battered: base flattened, gold scratched, a shard of emerald missing beside the Spartan helmet.

No longer flawless, but worth more than ever. A faint, guilty smile flickers on his lips.

Then he spots Lucas, sitting apart from the rest, his body slumped, his breath shallow.

He's taken the worst of them all.

ny moment now, they'll walk through that door.

Angie replays the conversation she just had with Nicole on the phone. She sits at the dining room table, startled at every sound, waiting for them to arrive. How long ago did she hang up? A minute? An hour? She can't keep track.

The front door handle rattles.

Her boys walk in. Their bruised faces downturned, dried blood streaking their features like a sort of macabre mascara. Frisco closes the door behind them as Lucas and Anthony plop down on opposite ends of the living room couch.

Angie bites her tongue at the dirt clinging to their clothes, now smearing onto her upholstery with a gritty scrape. Tonight, there's more than the grime they're tracking in to deal with.

Joseph trudges past, exhaling heavily, and disappears down the basement steps.

Michael engrossed in a televised wrestling match, barely glances up as Joseph hurries down the stairs.

"You just missed an awesome fight."

Joseph darts for the rear door. "No, I caught the fight."

The rasp in his cousin's voice pulls Michael's eyes away from the screen.

"What happened?" Michael takes in each new mark that wasn't on Joseph just half an hour ago.

"We just fought like fifty kids down the block."

Michael shrinks. "I missed it? How come you didn't get me?"

Joseph's expression shifts, Michael winces, regretting the words as soon as they leave his mouth, he knows he wouldn't have been much help.

Joseph moves past Michael, lowering his voice and parts the vertical blinds to peek outside.

"You see any kids down here?"

Michael shakes his head. "No."

"You hear anybody in the backyard?"

"No."

"Good. Come on, let's go upstairs."

It's not a request.

Angie pushes herself up from the table.

Frisco, hands shaking, fills a glass from the sink, water sloshing over the rim, and hands it to her. "Angie, you don't even understand. There were so many of them. I've never seen anything like that."

"I had everything under control," Lucas snaps, his voice rising as Joseph emerges from the basement door. "Until *he* showed up with his posse."

"I did what I had to," Joseph fires back.

Lucas springs up, adrenaline spiking through his veins. "What? Get my ass kicked?"

"First off, nothing was under control." The brothers face each other from across the room, tension crackling like two gunslingers waiting for the church bells to chime. "You're lucky we showed up when we did. Who knows how much worse it could've been?"

"Everything was fine until you started it!" Lucas's voice cracks under the weight of his own fury.

The house seems to shrink under the heat of their argument.

"Oh yeah? If I started it, how come they all kept going after and attacking you?"

Lucas leaps. "Because I was protecting you."

Joseph matches his movements.

"And then Anthony runs down like a psycho." Lucas fires off.

"Only because they were going to hit you!" Anthony shouts from the couch, his voice breaking as tears spill over.

The telephone cuts through the tension with a sharp ring.

All eyes snap to Angie as she grabs the receiver. She cups the bottom and glares at her sons. "Shut up, it's your father," she hisses.

The room falls silent, every eye on Angie.

Realizing she may have spoken too loudly, she softens her tone as she brings the phone back to her ear. "No, nothing's wrong."

She turns, her gaze passing over each of her sons. "The kids were in a fight."

Even from the kitchen, the boys can hear their father's voice, sharp and unintelligible through the receiver.

Frisco shuffles closer to Lucas, his hands fidgeting near his stomach.

Angie pauses, then continues. "It's over... Nothing, Joseph. Somebody took money from my purse, and they went looking for it."

She hesitates, lips pressing together as she chooses her next words.

Lucas sinks back onto the couch. Anthony pushes up, pacing the room.

"It's over now. Forget it... You don't have to leave work."

No goodbyes. No pleasantries.

The call ends. Angie hangs up.

"Was he mad?" Anthony asks.

Angie nods. A simple answer, enough to stop his pacing. "Oh boy."

Lucas grabs Frisco, pulling him close and shielding his words with a cupped hand.

Joseph hurries in. "What? What'd you just say?"

Frisco stiffens, his shoulders tensing.

Lucas, calmer now, tilts his head, the fight draining from his voice. "You didn't hit that kid first?"

It's a real question.

Joseph stops cold. The shift in Lucas's tone throws him off.

"No!" Joseph throws up his hands, his face flushing red. "What's the matter with you? I just went to war for you, and I get this shit?"

"I didn't see him hit that kid," Frisco blurts out, his head bouncing between the brothers.

Joseph's face twists in confusion, then anger. His temper explodes.

He lunges for the front door, ripping it open. "Get out of here."

Frisco freezes, stunned.

Joseph slams the door with a force that rattles the frame. Then yanks it open again.

"You didn't even throw one punch."

He slams it again, the sound echoing through the house.

Again, he flings it open. "Get out!"

Boom! Another violent slam.

"I didn't throw the first punch!"

"Joe, calm down," Frisco finally breaks through. "That's what I said. I know you didn't."

Joseph's shoulders slump, the fury leaking from him like steam off his skin. His face fades from bright red back to flesh.

"I'm sorry," he mutters. "I didn't hear. I thought you said I did."

Michael, who felt useless for missing the fight, seizes the moment. "Everybody just relax."

He leans in to kiss his aunt on the cheek and tosses Frisco his keys. "Come on, I'll get you to your car, and you guys can figure out what you're going to say when your dad gets home."

He hugs his cousins, then opens the door for Frisco. Frisco struggles to flash a smile for Angie, then pats Michael on the shoulder. "I tell you, it was so crazy, Lucas turned and hit me at some point."

They both laugh as they step outside.

Joseph, his sweat cooling on his skin, starts up the staircase, then pauses.

He sits.

Lucas, trailing behind, sits beside him. Their shoulders press together in the tight space.

"You alright?" Lucas asks.

"Yeah, I'm fine. Bruised my knee a little." Joseph lifts his knee, showing the torn denim, the raw scrape stained with gravel. "Took a shot in the back of the head, but I'm good."

"Okay. Good," Lucas says, satisfied.

Together they sit in silence, staring down the steps.

Waiting.

Listening.

For the next rattle of the doorknob.

For their father to return home.

Black trash bags, the only remnants of the block party, are stacked in orderly piles in front of each house. Cars settle back into their usual spots, and the quiet of Sinclair feels heavier than usual.

A pair of roving lights slices through the dark, swinging fast into Joseph's driveway.

Too fast.

The tires skid to a stop, kissing the edge where concrete meets grass.

Angie and her boys watch from the dining room table. The headlights' glow dims against the sheer curtains as the engine cuts off.

Joseph Sr. is home.

The stale air inside the house stiffens with unspoken words.

The front door bursts open, shattering the stillness.

Joseph flinches. His forearms prickle as a chill races down his spine. His father storms in, his polished leather shoes thudding like boots on the hardwood.

"I want the address of every last one of those bastards! How dare they steal from my house? Who were they?"

Joseph Sr. locks onto Lucas, crossing the room with surprising speed.

"Lucas! Who let them in here?"

Silence.

Angie tries to defuse. "Joseph, calm down. There were kids all over the block today."

Her words bounce off him like rain on a windshield.

"Did they have to come in my house? Do you think this would've happened if I was home?"

Rhetorical. The boys know better than to answer.

"No, of course it wouldn't, because I know better!"

Joseph Sr. pauses, glaring at each of them. Then he leans in, sniffing the air around Lucas.

"What? Were you drinking? Are you drunk!?"

He yanks Lucas up from his chair.

Lucas winces, but his father doesn't notice.

"Find out who they were. I'm going to kill every last one of those motherfuckers!"

Joseph Sr. waits for the usual pushback, a sarcastic remark, a protest.

But there is none.

Surprising their father, Joseph jumps in to defend Lucas.

"Dad, calm down."

Boom.

His father's palm slams against the table. Angie flinches, her hand quivering as she grips the table's edge. The whole thing shudders, but it holds.

"Don't tell me to calm down!" His blue eyes burn into each of his sons. "This is my family they crossed! Fuck them!"

Angie reaches for his hand, her voice rising in alarm. "Joseph, please. Your blood pressure. You're going to have a heart attack."

Joseph Sr. lets go, and Lucas slumps back into his seat, one hand clutching his ribs.

Their father storms into the kitchen. The rest of them sit frozen, listening to the faucet run.

He fills a glass, gulps the water down, wipes the excess droplets from his chin, then returns to the table.

His rage simmers into something quieter as he takes them in.

They've taken measures to clean up, scrubbed away the blood, and changed their clothes. But the evidence of the struggle remains.

He notices a cut below Anthony's eye, the bruise along Joseph's cheek, and the way Lucas grabs at his side, wincing with each breath.

Joseph Sr. pulls out a chair.

The chair's legs scrape the floor with a sound like nails on a chalkboard.

Then he sits down, his voice dropping low, almost to himself.

"I knew something was wrong. I just knew it."

Angie lies in bed, her eyes resting as she listens to the soft hum of running water from the bathroom. For the first time since the robbery, she allows herself to relax.

Joseph Sr. wipes a smattering of toothpaste from the counter, rinses his hands under the cold faucet, then switches off the light. He crosses into the bedroom and sits at the edge of the bed.

"You got home quickly," Angie states, her voice quiet.

"Yeah, well, I drove like a moron."

Angie opens her eyes ever so slightly, a quiet cue for her husband to slide under the covers beside her.

"I was upset," he admits.

Angie rests her head on his chest. His heartbeat, an erratic thumping beneath her ear, remains unsettled.

"Lucas blames Joseph," she whispers, "but I talked to Giuseppe, and he said it was a good thing Joseph came down when he did."

A short, dry laugh escapes Joseph Sr.

"What does Lucas know? He was drunk anyway. He'll come around."

She feels his heartbeat slow beneath her cheek.

Joseph Sr. lets out a long breath, his eyes drifting shut. "The boys stuck together when it counted, though. That's what's important."

"His friends said they never saw Anthony or Joseph like that." Angie closes her eyes again, relieved that tomorrow will be a new day. "I'm glad you're home."

Down the hall in the boys' bedroom, sleep has already settled in. Joseph rests peacefully on his mattress on the floor. Anthony, tucked under a light blanket, breathes steadily in his bed.

And in a perpendicular bed beside him, Lucas sprawls out, snoring, his usual basement crash pad reclaimed as simply a couch.

"In old Ohio there's a team
That's known throughout the land..."
-Ohio State University Fight Song

FIFTEEN

SUMMER COMMENCEMENT

Frisco closes the refrigerator door, a saran-wrapped plate of fried chicken cutlets in his hands. He sets the dish down in front of his brother, Gary.

"How do you play again?" Gary asks, eyeing the black cards spread across the table, the Loaded Questions logo staring back at him in stark white.

Frisco shoves a healthy portion of breaded cutlet into his mouth and starts explaining through his chewing. "You roll the dice, move your piece…" A burnt edge breaks off, an oily drip trailing down his chin. "…pick a card, ask the question on the card depending on what square you're on."

Jared winces at Frisco's mouthful of explanations and jumps in. "Then we write down our answers, and after I read them, you have to guess who said what."

"Yeah, if you hear 'I love Frisco's mother's chocolate chip potato,' you'd guess me." Anthony grins, taking over the explanation. "But if you hear 'I have a small penis,' then you'd know it was Lucas."

Lucas gives a languid shrug, smiling at the jab. *What could ya do?*

Joseph drops a bottle of ketchup in front of Frisco with a soft thud, who's already halfway through his second piece of chicken, then sits beside him. "Giuseppe, I'm glad you brought your brother around, it makes the jokes about your mother twice as funny."

Frisco, squirting a line of ketchup across a third cutlet, nods toward the family room. "So, you finally got your stuff put away, huh?"

"I had to. My sister's coming home this week, and she's got her own shit. Took a lot of work, but Lucas and Anthony helped."

Frisco lifts the last piece of cutlet to his mouth and takes a bite as Gary rolls the dice.

Game on...

The August sun scorches over Sinclair. Joseph Sr., a sweat line spreading across his chest, hoists the final suitcase into the back of the van.

"That's everything. Let's go."

The boys rush from the air-conditioned house and dive straight into the van's cool back seats, the sudden chill a relief from the heat. Angie locks the front door behind her and settles into the passenger seat, her pocketbook clutched in her lap.

"So, what is it?" Anthony asks as his father buckles in. "An eight-hour trip to Ohio State?"

Angie glances in the rearview mirror, nodding. "Yep."

Joseph leans against the window, pressing a pillow into the corner, shifting and adjusting but failing to get comfortable. "Should be fun."

"Oh yeah, can't wait," Lucas deadpans, his eyes rolling so far back they nearly disappear. "Wake me when we get there."

Joseph Sr. shifts the van into reverse, resting an arm across the back of Angie's seat as he inspects behind him.

Angie smiles as the boys erupt in unison: *"Mommy's getting her baby back! Mommy's getting her baby back!"*

The chant echoes through the van as it inches backward out of the driveway.

Stella sneaks Joseph into yet another place he doesn't belong.

Back in high school, she and her girlfriends would finagle her fifteen-year-old brother past doormen. They'd slip into Manhattan's club scene: pulsing lights, packed bodies, pounding bass. Now, she's found a way to plant him next to her in the student section at Ohio State's summer convocation.

Joseph stands among her soon-to-be ex-roommates, feeling out of place but grinning at Stella's achievement. Her smile widens, green eyes flashing with pride as she walks tall across the stage, her heels clicking with each step. She accepts her diploma with quiet grace, then jumps with joy, waving to the crowd. Confidence radiates from her as she jogs off the stage and into the raucous sea of fellow graduates.

"Can't wait to get home and see the rest of the family."

She wraps her arms around their mom. Their dad, his eyes glassy but composed, shakes hands with her nearby friends. Logan, the boyfriend who will be staying with them next month, flinches but tries to hide it as her father's handshake lingers a little too long, grip firm and deliberate.

With the ceremony behind them and farewells exchanged, the Vitaglianos pack up her belongings, squeezing everything and themselves into the overstuffed van for the long ride home.

Stella watches as the industrial smoke of New Jersey fades behind her, the van rolling over the Outerbridge.

Each passing landmark, every familiar road sign, sharpens her focus on the reality ahead; college is officially over.

Turning onto Sinclair Avenue, she takes in the familiar row of houses. Her fingers tap the seat, a quiet thrill building inside her.

The van eases into the driveway, tires crunching against the concrete, and Stella smiles.

One by one, they exit. Lucas, dodging the heavy lifting, shoots past the rest, unlocks the front, and dashes inside the house.

Joseph Sr. wrestles two suitcases clear, beginning the first of what will be many trips. Anthony and Angie each grab what they can.

Joseph and Stella bring up the rear.

At the door, Joseph holds it open, tipping his head toward her.

"Welcome home, sis."

Stella crosses over the threshold. Her smile lingers, a touch softer now.

Behind them, the door clicks shut, and a gray squirrel darts past, scampering up a nearby tree.

ACKNOWLEDGEMENTS

Some stories are patient. This was a particularly patient story. I'd be remiss not to thank the many folks who have known about this tale, asked about it, and at one point in its evolution were part of the film crew attached to it; *we'll get to that fun bit of trivia later*. First, I want to thank my mother, Lori Consolmagno, who was the very first person to read this story back in the early 2000s when it first came to life as a rushed screenplay. Next, I want to thank my father, Michael J. Sr., an artist in his own right, as well as my grandparents and siblings, Tara, Thomas, Christopher, Aaron, Gina, Tara Boccia and Jackie, from whom many acts and character moments in the story are inspired by their combined personalities. I'd also like to acknowledge a few friends, cousins, and extended family who inspired me. Since this will be in print, I'll simply say you know who you are, but to name a few, I am forever grateful to Uncle Bob, Aunt Florence, Uncle Tom, Aunt Theresa, Aunt Linda, Uncle Dave, Diego, Nicole, Michelle, Chris, Diana, Maria, Michael, Francis, Evan Stokes, Bryan Ponemon, Derrick Knorr, Anthony Coladonato, Michael Hitchcock, Frank Esposito, and the rest of the crew who humored me when I asked for their time. Some even jumping into freezing waters one frigid October afternoon to help film a summer pool scene.

I mentioned that this story began as a screenplay, and for a time, my only intention was to tell it in that medium. To that end, I'd like to give special thanks to my cousin David Larangeira, Michael Sammarco and filmmaking guru Marc Pitanza (whose book *STATEN ISLAND RAPID TRANSIT* is available on all platforms). These guys embarked on a wild journey with me as I attempted to create a movie without prior film experience and zero money. We never finished, but the footage we created together was, to be honest, pretty terrible; however, it was also earnest, and I wouldn't change it for anything.

Another Staten Island author and former neighbor who deserves thanks is Dawn Turizo (F.D.N. Wives), who put eyes on a very rough, very messy first draft as I began the transition from screenplay to full-blown narrative. To

Chris Carcich thank you for being a source of motivation while trying to squeeze in writing sessions during work hours. And a huge thank you to Amy Silver, and Tony Gasparro who were genuinely interested in my novel's progress and pushed me to complete the cover so it could be used on set as a piece of set dressing.

I'd like to conclude by thanking my wife, April, and our two children, Sofia Rayne and Michael J. the 3rd. Picking up a story set so long ago in the past, one that leans heavily on personal experience, has made me appreciate how wonderful it all turned out. This story never would have been finished without their support and understanding. I hope one day my children can look at what I have accomplished, (even if it only sells one copy), and understand that there isn't a time limit or gatekeeper that can stop you from reaching a goal. I love the life we are building together, and you inspire me every day.

Lastly, thank you, dear reader, for giving an unproven writer a chance to entertain you with this story. I hope it was worth the time you put into reading it, and if this one wasn't to your liking, I hope to wow you with the next one.

Michael J. Consolmagno Jr.

April 13, 2026

About The Author:

Michael J. Consolmagno Jr. is an emerging talent in contemporary storytelling, blending his New York roots with a passion for exploring life's transitions. Over the years, he's reinvented himself through careers in science, film, and now authorship; bringing a rich, multifaceted perspective to his work.

A lifelong creative, Michael's journey began with scribbling poetry in notebooks and crafting home-made graphic novels in his parents' basement, evolving into a deep commitment to narrative art. He currently lives in Staten Island, NY, with his wife and two children, where he continues to craft stories when not attending his son's soccer games or daughter's play rehearsals.

youtube.com/@greatcounsel

facebook.com/sifilmmaker

www.instagram.com/greatcounsel

www.x.com/sifilmmaker

www.tiktok.com/@michaeljosephconsolmagno